Quincy unlocked the passenger door for Lena. He looked over at her as he slowly opened it for her. She was about to step into the car when he suddenly grabbed her, halting her movement. When she turned to him, he pulled her into his arms and kissed her lips.

Lena was stunned at first, and her eyes widened in reaction to his aggressiveness. But she quickly relaxed and melted against him. When their lips parted, Lena looked up at him in a daze. She had never been kissed that way before. Quincy, too, was in a bit of a daze. He had not realized until then, just how much he really cared for her.

His embrace became more tender, and he placed his lips on hers for another kiss, this time parting her lips with his tongue. Lena placed her arms around him, squeezing him with all her might. This was the moment she had waited for all her life. On many occasions, Lena had dreamt about Quincy holding her in his arms and kissing her this way—so many times that the reality of it was staggering. She did not want to let him go.

Although it was dark and there were people moving about in the parking lot, Lena was oblivious to them. In the past, she would have been horrified at the thought of anyone witnessing her in this light, but now she did not care. She was in love with Quincy, and from the way he held her, Lena gleaned that he cared about her just as much.

BOOK YOUR PLACE ON OUR WEBSITE AND MAKE THE ARABESQUE ROMANCE CONNECTION!

We've created a customized website just for our very special Arabesque readers, where you can get the inside scoop on everything that's going on with Arabesque romance novels.

When you come online, you'll have the exciting opportunity to:

- View covers of upcoming books

- Learn about our future publishing schedule (listed by publication month and author)

- Find out when your favorite authors will be visiting a city near you

- Search for and order backlist books

- Check out author bios and background information

- Send e-mail to your favorite authors

- Join us in weekly chats with authors, readers and other guests

- Get writing guidelines

- AND MUCH MORE!

Visit our website at
http://www.arabesquebooks.com

FIRST LOVE

CHERYL FAYE

ARABESQUE
BET
BOOKS

BET Publications, LLC
www.bet.com
www.arabesquebooks.com

ARABESQUE BOOKS are published by

BET Publications, LLC
c/o BET BOOKS
One BET Plaza
1900 W Place NE
Washington, D.C. 20018-1211

First Printing: August, 2000

10 9 8 7 6 5 4 3 2 1
Printed in the United States of America

With undying devotion, I dedicate this story to the first man I've ever loved, my father, James Edward Smith, Sr. Thank you, Daddy, for being the sweetest, most loving father a girl could ever have.
I'm proud of you, too.

ONE

Lena Caldwell still had not gotten used to her mother not being there. At times she felt as if she no longer had a purpose in this world. She had taken care of her mother for so many years that now she felt useless.

Sadeira "Sadie" Caldwell had been an extraordinary seamstress. She used to work right out of her home because she was so good that her clients came to her. She'd taught Lena how to sew when Lena was still in junior high school. Sadie used to make all of her own clothes, and until Lena's sewing skills became so good that she could make her own, she also made Lena's.

Sadie had died of cancer three months ago. She had been diagnosed with an inoperable brain tumor four years earlier and told she would not live long afterward, but it took its sweet time killing her. Her condition had really begun to take its toll on her a year ago, and the last six months before her death had been very trying for Lena.

Lena had hired a nurse to come in and take care of her mother during the day, but in the evening she had been on her own. They could not afford to have Sadie stay in a hospital for an indefinite period of time, seeing as how there was nothing that could really be done for her anyway, so responsibility for her care had fallen on Lena.

Lena's father, Andrew Caldwell, had died two years earlier of a heart attack, and his insurance had just barely paid for his funeral—fortunately, he'd done a stint in the military when he was in his twenties, and that guaranteed him and his wife cemetery plots. Lena had been devastated by his sudden death. She and her father had always been very close. She had always been Daddy's little girl.

Lena had no real friends to speak of. She was an only child, and her parents had always been very strict about her comings and goings. They had not allowed her to date or accept telephone calls from boys until she was eighteen years old. With the kinds of restrictions that had been placed on her, there were really only two things that could have happened. She could have rebelled, in which case they would have had a wild child on their hands, or she could have obeyed them to the letter and not given in to peer pressure, thereby becoming something of a pariah. Lena had always been very obedient, so she became an outcast. She was far too shy to initiate any friendships on her own, and because of that she ended up being a loner.

She was very attractive, although there was nothing extraordinary about her looks. She never wore makeup on her nearly flawless, dark, cocoa-brown skin. In her teen years, her parents never allowed that. By the time Lena did not need their approval, she had gotten used to looking the way she did and felt no motivation to alter her looks, so she never bothered with such excesses. Her jet-black hair was long, and she still straightened it every weekend with a hot comb, as her mother had since she was a child. She usually wore it in a ponytail, because everything else took so much time. She had a small nose, which she thought was too flat, and a small mouth. When she smiled, she could brighten a room.

Lena used to attend church every Sunday, but when Sadie became too ill to attend she stopped going and stayed home with her. Sadly, after watching her mother suffer the way she had, Lena had somewhat lost her faith in God. She hadn't been back since.

Lena worked as a receptionist in the human resources department of a large New York City bank. Despite her shyness she was praised regularly by her superiors for the friendly and cheerful way she had of greeting visitors to the bank. She had held the position for three years, and although she was well-liked by everyone in the office she still kept to herself. She usually ate lunch alone, and more often than not she brought something from home as opposed to buying her lunch in the bank's cafeteria.

Since her mother's death, Lena had lived alone in the house where she had grown up. She knew everyone in the neighborhood, although she hardly ever said anything more than "hello" or "have a nice day" when she ran into any of her neighbors in the street.

Due to Lena's nonexistent social life, she spent a lot of her spare time sewing. She had a keen eye for style and fabric, and was always dressed impeccably. Just yesterday she had made the decision to move into what used to be her parents' bedroom and convert the smaller bedroom she used to sleep in into a sewing room. She still had her mother's old reliable Singer sewing machine.

Lena was also an avid reader. Although her taste in literature was quite varied, romance novels were counted among her favorites. On many occasions, Lena came home from work and—after eating dinner and washing the dishes—curled up on her sofa with a romance novel. She got more pleasure from fantasizing about being the heroine of a truly romantic story than she did from watching sitcoms or a movie.

In truth, the only thing Lena knew about romance was what she had read in her books. She was twenty-five years old, and had been on fewer dates than she could count on one hand. She had never even been French-kissed. Lena had pretty much resigned herself to the fact that she would probably die an old maid.

TWO

Quincy Taylor stood in front of his full-length mirror and carefully tied his new silk tie. Although it was only eight o'clock in the morning, his stereo was blasting one of his favorite CDs, Mint Condition's *Definition of a Band*. He figured, *What the hell.* His upstairs and downstairs neighbors were probably getting ready for work, anyway.

He had taken the day off from his regular job to go on an interview. He was currently employed as a headhunter at a prominent employment agency in Manhattan. Quincy was good at his job, too, but now he was looking for something better.

He'd gotten up that morning feeling pretty confident. His interview was for the position of Assistant Manager of Human Resources at one of the city's largest banks. The salary being offered was ten thousand dollars more a year than he was currently bringing home over his commission, and the benefits were exceptional. He figured that at thirty-three he had better start looking at the big picture. He would need health benefits if he ever decided to get married and have kids.

Quincy hoped that the job, if he got it, would be more stable than his current one. He had noticed that in the past six months a number of his coworkers had been let go suddenly. If they were letting people go who had been in the office for years and had seniority, what was to stop them from dismissing him? Also, he was the only African-American in the office. He was not willing to risk the chance that his race would be used against him.

He stepped over to his dresser and picked up the Givenchy Gentleman bottle and splashed some on. His suit jacket hung on the wooden valet at the foot of his bed. He grabbed it, put it on, then carefully stuffed an expertly folded square into his breast pocket and buttoned the top button of the jacket. He had decided to wear his lucky suit—the salt-and-pepper wool he had treated himself to for his birthday.

He stepped back in front of the mirror and checked his appearance. He smiled and said, "How can they tell you no?"

Quincy picked up his briefcase and checked to make sure his resumé was in his portfolio, and that he had his appointment and telephone books. He grabbed his wallet from the dresser top and checked the contents. As he stuffed it into his pants pocket, he decided to stop at the cash machine before he got on the subway to get a few dollars more.

He walked into the living room and turned his stereo off, then grabbed his overcoat and hat from the front closet and put them on. Still feeling confident as he left his apartment, Quincy told himself, *This job is mine.*

As he walked the three blocks to the subway, he smiled inwardly. On any other day Quincy might have ignored a not-so-pretty woman he passed, but today he greeted one pleasantly and with sincerity, and her smile of appreciation made him feel even better.

The cash machine was a block from the subway station, and after he stopped to get a little extra cash Quincy headed straight there. Before he got on the train, he stopped at a newsstand and bought the paper. The first thing he did was check his horoscope.

He was a Capricorn. His birthday was January third. According to his horoscope he would meet someone very special today who would initiate a positive chain of events in his life.

He smiled. That had to be this guy, Dave Patterson, who was interviewing him today.

Yeah, he thought, *this job is mine.*

THREE

Lena had just hung up the telephone when she saw a handsome stranger step off the elevator. As he strode confidently toward the reception desk, she could not help admiring him. He was about six feet tall, she guessed. His skin was the color of honey. He wore a very stylish gray fedora, and before he opened his mouth to say a word he removed it from his head. His dark brown hair was neatly cut in a short fade. His eyes were bright and friendly, and he had the cutest pug nose. Lena noticed that his small ears stuck out a bit, but that only added to his debonair good looks. The only hair on his face was a neatly trimmed mustache that more than complemented his sensuous lips.

"Good morning," he said cheerfully, and then he smiled.

She immediately noticed that his teeth were beautiful. "Good morning. May I help you?" Lena asked, and she smiled in return.

"Yes. I have a nine-thirty appointment with Dave Patterson. My name is Quincy Taylor."

"Okay, Mr. Taylor. Please have a seat and I'll let Mr. Patterson know that you're here."

"Thank you." Quincy stepped over to the

comfortable looking leather sofa and sat down. He rested his briefcase on the seat beside him.

Lena picked up her phone and dialed a number.

"Hi, Grace. Could you let Dave know that Quincy Taylor is here to see him? Thank you."

When she hung up she said, "Mr. Taylor, Mr. Patterson will be right with you. Can I take your coat?"

"Oh, yes, thank you."

He stood up and removed his coat as Lena got up from her chair to take it from him.

As he handed his coat and hat to her, he smiled and said, "Thank you very much."

"You're welcome."

Lena thought he looked very smart in his double-breasted suit. She briefly wondered if he was interviewing for the assistant manager position that just recently opened up.

Quincy returned to his seat on the sofa and smiled as he watched the young sister hanging up his coat. He thought she was very pretty.

Lena was wearing a black wool skirt with a hem that stopped just above her knee, a white blouse, and a black-and-white hounds-tooth check jacket. The blouse was fastened at the neck with a decorative gold button. Her jet-black hair was pulled back and worn in a ponytail that fell past her shoulders. Although she was a small woman—he guessed no more than five-feet two or three inches tall, and probably ninety pounds soaking wet—he could tell that she had a nice figure.

"Excuse me, but can you tell me if there have

been many people interviewing for the assistant manager position?" Quincy asked her out of the blue.

"Oh, I really don't know," she explained with an apologetic smile. "Sorry."

"That's okay. I was just curious." After a brief silence he said, "I'm interviewing for the position myself."

"Oh. Well, I wish you luck," she offered.

"Thanks."

At that moment a woman entered the reception area from the offices in back. "Mr. Taylor?"

"Yes," he said, as he reached for his briefcase and rose from his seat.

"Mr. Patterson will see you now."

Quincy followed the woman out of the reception area. As he passed Lena, he whispered, "Keep your fingers crossed."

"Okay," she said with a smile. She held up both hands, with fingers crossed.

"Thanks."

Once Quincy Taylor was gone, Lena smiled as she thought about what a pleasant personality he seemed to have. She genuinely hoped he would get the job. It would be nice to have someone as handsome and as pleasant as he was to look at every morning.

FOUR

Quincy's interview with Dave Patterson lasted for almost three hours. While he was there he also met with the head of human resources, as well as the woman whose position he would be taking over if he got the job.

By the time the interview was over, he had a very good feeling about the whole meeting. His prospective employers had made the whole process very informal. They appeared to be very enthusiastic about his past work history, and his attitude in general. He was fairly positive they would be calling him in a day or two to make him an offer.

Dave Patterson walked him out to the reception area when the interview was over, and they said their good-byes there.

When Lena saw Quincy shaking hands with Dave, she got up and went to the closet to retrieve his coat and hat.

After Dave Patterson had walked out of the area, Quincy turned toward Lena; he was smiling.

"How did it go?" she asked.

"Very well, I think," he said happily as he took his things from her.

"That's good."

He was putting on his coat when he said, "I think you brought me good luck."

"Me?" she said, blushing as she moved back to her desk to sit down.

"Yes, you. As soon as I stepped off that elevator and saw you sitting there, I said to myself, 'that sister's going to bring you good luck, Quincy.' "

"Well . . ." she stammered. She quietly thanked God for making her skin so dark, because she suddenly felt very flushed. "No one's ever told me that before."

"No? I'm surprised. I guess that's why they have you sitting out here, though. I'm sure you make a lot of people feel at ease when they come in here to interview," Quincy said as he stood at her desk.

"Thank you," she said shyly, not knowing what else to say.

"Well, I hope I'll be seeing you again in a couple of weeks on my starting day," Quincy said with a chuckle as he started back to the elevator bank.

Suddenly, he stopped, turned to her, and asked, "By the way, what's your name?"

"Lena Caldwell," she said softly.

He stepped back to her desk and offered his hand. "Pleased to meet you, Lena Caldwell."

She shook his hand and knew right away that her knees would have buckled beneath her if she had been standing.

"It's nice to meet you, too," she said timidly as she cast her eyes down.

Being very astute when it came to the opposite sex, Quincy noticed her meekness immediately. He smiled because he knew that it was not a flirtatious ploy. "See you soon, Lena," he said, and turned back toward the elevators to leave.

Her heartbeat had tripled when she touched his hand, but she managed to whisper, "Bye."

FIVE

When Lena got off the train in the Bronx that evening after work, she really did not feel like cooking, so she stopped at the Chinese restaurant near the subway exit and ordered a dish to go.

When she got home she turned on her stereo and put on a Babyface tape before she even took off her coat. She loved to listen to his songs. Aside from the beauty of the music, she thought his words were the most sensitive and romantic she had ever heard.

As she ate her dinner of shrimps with lobster sauce, she thought about Quincy Taylor. She really hoped he would get the job.

She liked him, although she was sure that he hadn't had another thought about her after he walked out of the doors of the bank. Her imagination was running wild, picturing a man like Quincy Taylor as her boyfriend, but she could not help what she was feeling. No man had ever said anything so sweet to her before. *Did he really think I would bring him good luck, or was he just teasing me?*

What the heck, she thought, *it doesn't matter, any-*

way. For the moment, she was enjoying the little bit of attention he had given her. Lord only knew when she would receive so much attention from a man again.

Quincy did not get home that afternoon until almost four-thirty. Instead of going straight home when he left the bank, he had called his best friend, Serge Kinnard, and met him for a late lunch.

To his surprise, Serge had taken the liberty of inviting two of his coworkers to join them. They were two very attractive ladies, and sharing a meal with them made the whole lunch scene very enjoyable. He could tell that one of them was interested in him, but he did not pursue her. Quincy decided it would be best if he spoke to Serge first to get a little feedback on her before deciding to make any moves.

They were at the restaurant for almost two hours, and the ladies very generously picked up the tab. When Quincy left them, he stopped in a nearby record store and purchased a couple of CDs to add to his already extensive collection at home.

By the time he arrived at his apartment later that afternoon, Quincy was feeling unusually carefree. He walked over to the stereo and turned it on, then placed the new R. Kelly disc he had just purchased on the machine before he had even removed his coat and hat. He turned the volume up loud.

He removed his hat, but took his time taking

off his coat because he was busy scanning his mail—bills, bills, and more bills. He threw the pile on the end table.

He stepped over to the telephone and noticed that there was a message on the answering machine. He pressed the rewind button.

As he hung his coat in the closet, he half-listened to the message play back. The only part of the message he caught was "Patterson." He hurriedly closed the closet door, moved back to the answering machine to turn up the volume, and pressed the rewind button.

"Hello, Quincy. This is Dave Patterson of City-wide Bank. I'd really appreciate it if you could give me a call this afternoon or tomorrow morning. I'll be at the office today until five. My number is three four oh, seven eight hundred, extension twenty-five."

Quincy immediately looked at his watch. Four thirty-five. He picked up the telephone and hurriedly dialed the number. He stretched the cord of the telephone across the living room to turn down the volume of his stereo.

"Extension twenty-five," Quincy said when the call was answered.

After a couple of seconds he heard, "Dave Patterson."

"Dave, hello. This is Quincy Taylor."

"Hello, Quincy. Thanks for returning my call so quickly. I was calling because I've spoken with everyone here and we're all in agreement that you're the best-qualified candidate we've talked to. I'd like to offer you the position of human resources assistant manager," Dave Patterson said.

Quincy was beaming and silently mouthed, *"Yes!"* before he responded, "Thank you, Dave. I accept."

"Great. I know you probably have to give your current employer notice, but we were hoping you would be able to start on March eighth," Dave said.

"Hold on a minute, Dave, let me check my calendar," Quincy said as he reached for his briefcase. He hurriedly yanked the book out of his briefcase and carelessly let the bag drop to the floor. He opened the appointment book and checked the date. "March eighth is fine. I can start then."

"That's great. We'll need you to come in before that, maybe one day this week on your lunch hour, to take the mandatory drug test, but other than that the job is yours."

"That's great. Thank you very much. I can come in tomorrow if that's all right with you," Quincy offered.

"That's fine. You can go straight to our medical department. That's on the seventeenth floor. It should take all of ten minutes."

"Okay. I'll do that."

"Great. As soon as we get the results of the test, I'll send you a confirmation letter," Dave said.

"That's fine," Quincy said.

"Well then, I'll see you on the eighth," Dave Patterson said.

"Definitely," Quincy said, with a big smile.

"And thanks again, Dave. I look forward to working with you."

"Likewise, Quincy. Have a good evening."

"Thank you. You do the same."

When Quincy hung up the telephone, he shouted in delight. He turned his stereo up and began blasting his music once again.

He was ecstatic. A ten thousand dollar raise. His mind was working overtime, thinking about all the things he would do with the new money.

He could not wait to get to work tomorrow to tell his boss. He really wanted to tell him where to get off, but knew better than to burn his bridges. He would go in there and play the role for them, but he was also going to tell them that he had to leave this coming Friday, as opposed to the two weeks Dave Patterson had allowed for.

Quincy was going to take a week for himself.

He had originally planned to cook a steak for dinner, but decided that a celebration was called for. He picked up the telephone and dialed a number.

"This is Mayella Richardson. Can I help you?"

"Hey, sexy," he said in a soulful voice.

"Quincy?"

"The one and only."

"Oh my goodness! I haven't heard from you in ages. How the hell are you?"

"I'm fine, May. How've you been?"

"I've been okay. To what do I owe the pleasure of this call?" she asked coyly.

"What are you doing tonight?"

"I don't have anything planned. Why? What do you have in mind?"

"Well, I was wondering if you'd like to join me for an impromptu celebration," he said with a smile.

"What are we celebrating?"

"My new job."

"Oh? Where?" she asked with genuine interest.

"At Citywide Bank. I'm the new assistant manager of their human resources department," Quincy said smugly.

"Really? Congratulations! That's great!"

"Yeah, thanks. So, would you care to share in my celebration?"

"Well, is this going to be an all-nighter, or what?"

"Have you got all night?"

"For you I do."

Quincy's chest puffed out even more. "Then we can make it an all-nighter."

"Where are you?" Mayella asked.

"I'm home. You get off at five-thirty, right?"

"Yup."

"How about I come and pick you up from work, and we can start from there," Quincy told her.

"That sounds good."

"Great. So I guess I'll see you at five-thirty."

"I'm looking forward to it," she cooed.

"Me, too."

After Quincy hung up, he went straight to his bedroom closet and retrieved a suit and shirt and his garment bag. Since he had not yet changed his clothes, he decided to keep on the suit he was wearing. He packed the bag with his underwear and cologne and other toiletries and smiled as he thought about the night ahead of him.

He was glad he had a friend like Mayella. They had known each other for almost ten years, having met at the birthday party of a mutual friend. Over the years they had occasionally gotten together for brief physical encounters, but had mutually, although nonverbally, agreed that a commitment was not for them.

He was still feeling very lucky. He started to think about his horoscope for that day. It had definitely been on the money. Dave Patterson was certainly the first link in that positive chain of events he had read about. He also thought about that girl, Lena, the receptionist at the bank. He smiled as he thought about her reaction when he told her she had brought him good luck. He could not remember the last time he had seen a woman in New York City actually blush without trying to be coy.

He thought she was cute. No, he thought, she was more than cute—she was fine—but as soon as he'd gotten just a little bit personal she seemed to retreat into a shell, as if she were afraid of the world. For reasons he could not explain, that turned him on a lot. But Quincy had never been involved with a woman who was afraid to ask for what she wanted. Admittedly, he was attracted to women who were assertive and a bit uninhibited. That was what he liked about Mayella. She did not mince words, and she was not the least bit shy.

As he zipped up his garment bag and lifted it off the bed, he smiled in anticipation. It would no doubt be a night to remember.

SIX

Two weeks later . . .

Lena was at work early that Monday morning. The department heads of the bank were having their quarterly meeting in the main conference room, which was located just outside of human resources. The office manager had asked Lena to come in at eight, since the meeting started at eight-thirty. Lena did not mind. She could use the overtime.

The vice president of human resources was very nice to her, too. Since she had arrived so early, he invited her to help herself to the breakfast that was being served at the meeting. So before everyone got there, Lena went in and took a bagel with cream cheese, a blueberry danish, and a cup of coffee.

It was a quarter to nine, and she had just bent down under her desk to pick up a crumpled napkin that had missed the trash can. When she sat up, she was surprised to see Quincy Taylor standing at her desk. He was wearing a big beautiful smile.

"Good morning," he said.

"Good morning." The surprise at seeing him clearly showed on her face.

"I told you you'd bring me good luck."

Lena smiled shyly. She was speechless.

"Today is my first day," he said.

"Con . . . congratulations," she finally managed to say as she blushed uncontrollably.

"Thank you. Lena . . . Caldwell, right?"

"Yes." She was shocked, but totally thrilled, that he remembered.

"Do you remember mine?"

How could I forget? "Yes. Quincy Taylor. Right?"

"I'm supposed to report to Dave Patterson. Is he in?"

"Oh, yes. I'll call him," she said as she nervously turned to the phone.

Lena knew Dave Patterson's extension by heart, but for some reason her mind went blank and she could not think of it. She picked up the telephone directory and quickly skimmed it, looking for his number. Quincy stood over her the entire time.

When she finally dialed the number, Dave Patterson picked up the call.

"Hi, Dave. Quincy Taylor is here."

"Thank you, Lena."

"All right." As she hung up she told Quincy, "He'll be right out."

"Thank you," he said with a charming smile.

Her heart was racing. She could not believe he was actually there. She had thought about him so many times in the past two weeks. She had actually prayed that he would get the job. Now, here he was.

Lena was nervous as he continued to stand at her desk. She felt as though her thoughts were readable, that he knew all the different things she had thought about him.

"That's a very unique pin you're wearing," Quincy suddenly said.

On the lapel of her jacket, Lena wore a gold-colored pin in the design of an African mask. "Thank you." She sighed.

"Quincy! How are you?" Dave Patterson asked as he entered the reception area. He immediately offered his hand.

Quincy shook it and said, "I'm fine, Dave. How are you?"

"Fine. Come on back," Dave said, leading Quincy away from her.

"See ya, Lena," Quincy said as they walked away.

"Bye."

Finally, she was able to exhale. She felt beads of sweat bursting out on her forehead. *Did he notice?* she wondered.

She felt a little bit foolish because she had become so flustered. *He must think I'm pathetic.* Lena wished she had the nerve to look him straight in the eye and compliment him the way he had complimented her, but she knew she would never have that much confidence in herself. She hated being such a coward.

SEVEN

Cheryl Stewart was sitting in her office when Dave Patterson passed by with the fine brother who had interviewed for an assistant manager position a couple of weeks ago. She immediately picked up the telephone and began to dial.

As she listened to the phone ring, she glanced at her reflection in the small makeup mirror she kept on her desk and ran her hand across her puffed out weave, making sure there were no hairs out of place.

"Bernadette King," a voice said.

"Hey, Bernie, this is Cheryl. Remember that fine brother that interviewed for Casey's spot?"

"Yeah."

"He got the job," Cheryl said.

"Get outta here!"

"Yeah. He just passed by my office with Dave."

"Well, go 'head, brotha!" Bernadette cheered. "Are you going to go over and introduce yourself?" She already knew she would.

"Of course I am. I wanna make the brother feel welcome, you know. Help him get acclimated."

"Yeah, I bet. He's probably married with kids."

"Like I care," Cheryl said disparagingly.

"Yeah, I know you don't. Why don't you invite him out with us this Friday?" Bernadette suggested.

"You know, I was thinking about that, but I think I'll have Reggie ask him so it doesn't seem like I'm trying to push up on him just yet."

"Yeah, and he'd probably be more inclined to hang out with Reggie than with one of us, anyway, considering that he doesn't know us yet."

"Yeah. But I'ma go over and introduce myself and welcome him to the bank. You know, like a good coworker should," Cheryl said facetiously.

"Hmph. Miss Model Employee, you are somethin' else," Bernadette said with a chuckle.

"I'll talk to you later."

"See you at lunchtime."

"Yeah, okay. Bye."

Cheryl was a senior benefits coordinator at the bank. She had been employed there for fifteen years. She was a thirty-six-year-old divorcee, and the mother of two teenage sons. She was a very stylish dresser, although she often came to work in outfits that were not suitable for the office. She could be quite boisterous at times, too, and was not one to bite her tongue when she had something to say and she wanted people to hear her. Cheryl was good at her job, and because of that her aggressive personality was often overlooked. Her face was always heavily made up, but never unbecoming. Her long nails were always perfectly manicured and brightly polished, usually in multicolored designs. Cheryl's hair was currently weaved, with a full head of curls flowing down her back, but she was very fickle when it came to hairstyles. One day she would wear a weave, the next a short bob. She was not above wearing a wig to suit her mood, either.

Since the outer wall of her office was actually a pane of glass, Cheryl had noticed Quincy Taylor the day he came in be to interviewed. Being that Cheryl often placed more value on outward appearance than inner beauty, she was immediately attracted to Quincy because of the way he dressed and carried himself. She had noticed, too, his doubletake and mischievous smile when he spotted her. She was certain that once he got to know her they would become good friends. Very good friends, if Cheryl had her way.

EIGHT

By noon Quincy had met the administrative assistant assigned to work with him. She was an Hispanic woman by the name of Maritza Perez. Quincy liked her bubbly personality right off.

He had taken care of all of his administrative business and had settled into his office when—as he was about to pick up the telephone to call Serge—a brother he had never seen before walked into his office after tapping lightly on the door.

"How you doin'?" he asked with uncommon familiarity. He walked in as if he belonged there. "I'm Reggie McFadden. I work down the hall, in benefits." He offered his hand.

Quincy rose from his seat and shook Reggie's hand as he said, "Hey, what's up? Quincy Taylor."

"It's nice to meet you, Quincy. I'm glad to see a brother got this position. There's only a handful of us here, and you're the first one in management."

"Yeah?" Quincy was glad to have that bit of information, but he thought it was quite presumptuous of Reggie McFadden to automatically assume that they were "homeboys." "How long have you been here?" Quincy covertly sized Reggie up.

"Goin' on four years," Reggie answered smugly.

"So, it's not that bad, huh?"

"It has its moments, just like any place."

"Yeah, I heard that." Having been a recruiter for so many years, Quincy was well aware of the politics in corporate America, especially for a black man.

"You got plans for lunch?" Reggie then asked.

"No, I don't."

"Why don't you join me and a couple of the sisters that work here in the department for lunch?" Reggie offered.

"Hey, that sounds like a plan. What time?" Quincy asked.

"One o'clock."

"All right, I can do that."

"We usually meet at the elevator."

"All right, Reggie. I'll see you at one."

"Later," Reggie said. Then he turned and walked out.

Quincy smiled as he sat down behind his desk. Reggie seemed like a nice enough guy, even though Quincy thought he was a bit forward. But he had to agree with Reggie on one thing— it was nice to see another brother.

Suddenly, Quincy rose from his desk and walked to the door. He stepped out to speak to his assistant. "Maritza, what time do you go to lunch?" he asked.

"I usually go at twelve-thirty. Do you want me

to change that?" she asked with a smile that Quincy knew was phony.

"No. No, don't change your lunchtime. If that's what time you've been going, then by all means continue. I'm not here to disrupt things," Quincy said. "We have voice mail, right?"

"Yes."

"All right. I'll be going out at one. I should be back by two, two-thirty."

"All right, Quincy," she said gingerly, waiting to see how he would respond to her using his first name as opposed to Mr. Taylor.

"Have a good lunch," he said with a smile.

"Thank you, Quincy," Maritza said, smiling genuinely this time. "You, too."

Lena was sitting alone in the cafeteria, eating her homemade lunch of meat loaf, spicy rice, and collard greens, when she spotted Quincy Taylor. He was with Reggie McFadden, Cheryl Stewart, and Bernadette King. She tried to act as if she had not seen them, and quickly put her head down as if she were concentrating on her food.

It was disheartening for her to see Quincy with them. She had always gotten the feeling that they overlooked her on purpose, since they had never offered any type of friendship in the years she had been at the bank. She hoped Quincy would not be negatively influenced by their standoffish ways and decide that he, too, had no time for her.

* * *

Quincy was surprised to see Lena in the cafeteria alone when he walked in with Reggie, Cheryl, and Bernadette. He tried to get her attention when he first noticed her, but she would not look his way. She was sitting too far away for him to call out to her, especially since this was his first day on the job. He could not, and would not, make a spectacle of himself for anyone.

As he turned toward the table where his lunchmates were seated, he realized that he was glad to know that Lena also took her lunch break at one o'clock. He decided right away that he would ask her to have lunch with him some time.

During his encounter with Reggie, Cheryl, and Bernadette, Quincy learned a good little bit about the bank and how it treated its employees. Between the three of them, there were about twenty-seven years of experience. Aside from Lena, they were the only four blacks in the human resources department at Citywide.

Realizing that, Quincy briefly wondered why Lena was not a part of this little clique. He almost asked them about it, but decided that he would rather hear it from Lena.

Before lunch was over Cheryl reached across the table and touched his hand. "What are you doing after work Friday, Quincy?" she asked with a soft smile. He had not missed the coy looks she had been throwing his way the whole hour.

"I don't have any plans," he told her, looking her squarely in the eye.

"We're all going to this club called Vibrations

after work. It's free for ladies before seven o'clock, and there's a free buffet, which is really a full dinner. Why don't you come with us?"

"Vibrations? I've heard of that place, but I've never been there," Quincy told her honestly.

"So why don't you come? It's always jumpin'—right, Reggie?" Cheryl asked, looking for help with persuading Quincy.

"Yeah, they be jammin' in there. Most definitely. And the ladies . . . man, the ladies be in there," Reggie said to Quincy with a conspiratorial nod of his head.

Quincy smiled at Reggie and said, "Yeah? Well, maybe I will join you. As a matter of fact, I'll call a couple of my people and we can make it a hang."

Reggie and Quincy slapped each other five as Reggie said, "That's a bet. The more the merrier."

On Friday of that same week, upon his return from lunch with his best friend Serge, Quincy stopped at the reception desk to speak to Lena. "And how've you been, Miss Lena?" he asked with a smile.

Lena's normally bubbly work persona always ran for cover around Quincy, and her timidness moved to the fore. She answered shyly, "Fine, thank you. I have two messages for you."

"Oh, thank you."

As he scanned the messages briefly, he asked her, "Did you go out at lunchtime? It's beautiful outside."

"No, I stayed in today."

"Oh. That's too bad. But spring is definitely on its way," he said.

"That's good to know. I'll be glad when I can take off my heavy coat," Lena said with a light chuckle. Quincy had a way of making her feel at ease, despite how nervous his presence always made her initially.

"Yeah, I know what you mean."

"So how was your first week?" she suddenly asked.

He smiled at her for asking. "It was good," he said thoughtfully. "Yeah, it was good. Very interesting," he added as he nodded his head.

"That's good," she said, but could not reciprocate the bold look he gave her.

"Well, let me get back there and see what they've got waiting for me. I'll talk to you later, Lena."

"Okay, bye," she said with a shy smile.

"Bye," he said flirtatiously, and winked at her.

NINE

Three more weeks had passed, and Quincy was feeling very good in his new position at the bank. He had developed a good relationship with Maritza; they worked well together. He had told her from the beginning that he wanted her to be honest about her feelings regarding the way he worked, because he would always be honest about what he expected of her.

He had come to know quite a bit about his new associates, Cheryl and Reggie. He had noticed right away that Bernadette was the quiet one of the bunch. Unlike Cheryl, she was very discreet about her private life. She had a habit of sitting back and letting her two cohorts do all the talking. Quincy learned that Reggie, a very immature twenty-eight year old, fancied himself a ladies' man. He was always talking about some woman he had gotten over on.

Cheryl was just a big flirt. When he thought about it he always smiled, because she was so obvious. She did not even try to camouflage her interest. Quincy knew he could have acted on her advances any number of times, but he had made up his mind from the start that he would not even go there. He figured she was just too easy. Besides, he could not stand all that makeup. There was nothing he liked less than hugging up with a woman only to draw back and find makeup all over his clothes. He could see that she would be very pretty if she did not wear so much of it. And the fake hair; he had nothing against a few extensions, if that was what a woman wanted to do for herself, but the wild weave look just did not cut it with him.

They were all right to hang out with sometimes, though. He just had to remind himself not to take them too seriously.

In the next moment, Reggie came into his office.

"Hey, Q, what's up?"

"What's up, Reg?"

"Ain't nothin'," Reggie flopped down in one of Quincy's chairs. "You hangin' tonight, right?"

"Yeah, I'm gonna hang for a while."

Reggie smiled conspiratorially as he leaned forward in the chair and said, "I know you noticed how Cheryl's been pushing up on you, man."

"Yeah, I've noticed," Quincy said, disinterested.

"So what you gonna do, man? You gonna hit that?"

Quincy was a bit surprised by his question. He huffed and said, "Hey, Reggie, she doesn't do anything for me."

"Nah? Man, I think Cheryl's fine!"

"Yeah? Well, why aren't you hittin' it?" Quincy asked sarcastically.

"Hey, man, don't think I haven't tried. But she ain't wit' it."

"Yeah, well, neither am I. But you know what I've been wondering? How come y'all never invite Lena out with y'all?"

Reggie laughed and said, "You're kiddin', right? Man, Lena don't be hangin' out. She's a straight up church girl. Besides that, she's afraid of her own shadow. Could you really see her hangin' out with us? I don't think so."

"Have you ever asked her?" Quincy said softly. Suddenly, his already low opinion of Reggie hit the floor.

"I don't have to. Have you ever talked to her?" Reggie asked, looking at Quincy as if he were crazy.

"Yes, I have. I don't see anything wrong with her."

Reggie chuckled and said, "Man, I'm tellin' you. She don't hang. If you don't believe me, why don't you ask her? Tell me what she says."

"I will."

"Tell me what she says," Reggie repeated.

Later that day, Quincy was returning from the men's room when he walked past the glass partition that separated the reception area from the rest of the department. He turned into the reception area and approached Lena's desk.

"Hi, Lena."

Due to the fact that her back was to him, she had not seen him approach. She turned quickly in her seat, recognizing his voice.

"Hi, Quincy."

"How are you doin'?"

"Fine, thanks."

"You know what I wanted to ask you? What are you doing this evening?"

She blushed and said, "Nothing."

"Reggie, Cheryl, Bernadette, and I are going dancing this evening. Why don't you come with us?"

She was stunned. They had never invited her to go out with them. *Why all of a sudden?* she wondered. "Oh, no, thank you. I can't," she said hesitantly.

"Why not? You just said you weren't doing anything," he said with a questioning smile.

"I don't dance," she said shyly. "I mean, I don't know how to dance."

Quincy did not know what to say at first. He just stood there, leaning on the edge of her desk, and looked at her with a curious smile. *She's serious,* he thought. *She really doesn't know how to dance.*

"I'll teach you."

"No, thank you. That's okay," she said with downcast eyes.

He could not explain it—because he had never had the experience before—but at that very moment he became so turned on by her that he wanted to grab her and stretch her out across her desk and make mad passionate love to her.

"Well, then, why don't we have lunch one day next week?" he asked.

She looked up at him in surprise. He smiled tenderly at her. Lena fell in love with him in that instant.

"But don't you usually go to lunch with Reggie?" she asked bashfully.

"Well, to be perfectly honest with you, I go to lunch with whomever I choose to go to lunch with, if they'll go with me," he said, as he stared into her eyes. "Will you?"

Lena could not help but blush. Then she said softly, "Yes."

"Great. Any particular day?" he asked.

"No. It doesn't matter."

"Okay. Well, we can talk about that next week." He stood at his full height and took a step back.

"Okay."

"Have a good weekend, Lena, if I don't see you again today," Quincy said sincerely.

"Thank you, Quincy. You, too. And thanks for asking me."

"Anytime, Lena. Anytime."

When Quincy left the reception area, Lena's face broke into a big smile. *He likes me.*

TEN

Lena and Quincy met for lunch that next Wednesday. Being the genuinely naive woman that she was, she had not realized that he wanted to take her out to a restaurant, so she had brought her lunch from home. That being the case, they ended up eating in the cafeteria.

Lena was truly embarrassed that she had misunderstood his intentions. "I'm sorry, Quincy, that I messed up your lunch plans," she said softly as he joined her with his tray.

He looked at her with raised eyebrows and countered, "You didn't mess up anything Lena. My plan was to have lunch with you, and that's what we're doing. I just thought we could do it outside, but this is okay."

"I misunderstood you."

"That's all right. What you're eating looks a lot better than this, or probably anything we could have gotten outside, anyway. I bet you're a great cook, huh?" he said with a friendly smile.

"I wouldn't say that. I'm really not that good. I wouldn't subject anyone else to my cooking," she said modestly.

"Aw, come on, I can see you're not that bad."

"My mother taught me how to cook, but I doubt if I'll ever be as good as she was."

"Do you live with your parents?" he asked as he placed a forkful of food in his mouth.

She lowered her head and answered, "My parents are dead. I live alone."

"Oh, I'm sorry."

"That's all right."

They were quiet for a few seconds until Lena broke the silence. "My father died of a heart attack a few years ago. I just lost my mother about four months ago. She had cancer," she said softly.

"I'm sorry."

"That's all right. They're both in a better place now."

Quincy was beginning to feel a little uncomfortable talking about her parents' deaths. He tried to lighten the mood. "So, Lena, since you can't dance, what do you like to do for fun? Do you go to the movies much?"

"No. I don't really go out a lot. I'm more of a homebody."

"Is that by choice?"

Lena did not know what to say at first. *What should I tell him, that I don't have any friends to go to the movies with? Should I tell him that I don't have the nerve to go to the movies by myself?*

"I guess," she finally answered. "I don't really know a lot of people. My parents were always really strict about me having company and everything while I was growing up."

"Would you like to go to the movies?"

She looked across the table at him as butterflies fluttered around in her stomach. *Is he asking me for a date?* "When?" she asked softly.

"Anytime. Tonight, if you like."

"Oh, I can't tonight. I . . . I have something to do this evening," she lied.

"Well, what about Friday, then? Are you busy Friday evening?"

"No," she said, swallowing deeply.

"Then how about we take in a movie Friday night?"

He is asking me for a date. Her heart began to race.

"All right," she answered. "What time?"

"Right after work. We can go straight from here, if you don't mind."

"No, I don't mind," she said, and she smiled bashfully at him.

"Good, then we have a date."

A date, she thought. *Quincy Taylor actually asked me out.* Just then, Reggie, Cheryl, and Bernadette walked over to their table.

"Hey, Quincy. Hi, Lena," Cheryl said with an exaggerated air.

"Hey. What's up, y'all?" Quincy responded.

"Hi," Lena said, embarrassed about being caught alone with Quincy.

"We're going out by the park," Cheryl volunteered. "Why don't y'all come out with us?"

"Maybe a little later, Cheryl," Quincy said.

"We'll be near the fountain," Reggie said, and he patted Quincy on his shoulder.

"All right. See you later."

Once they had left Lena asked, "Do you want to go outside with them?"

"Why? Do you?"

"No. I was just going to say if you wanted to go with them, it was all right," she offered generously.

He smiled at her and said, "No. I'm where I want to be."

She blushed and lowered her eyes.

Much later that afternoon, as Lena made preparations to go home, she left the reception desk to go to the ladies' room. She was in one of the stalls when she heard Cheryl and Bernadette enter the bathroom.

"Well, Quincy don't know it yet, but Friday night he's going home with me. I've gotten rid of the boys for that night, and I plan on having a very exciting evening with him, if you know what I mean," Cheryl said with a boisterous laugh.

Bernadette joined in and said, "I know exactly what you mean. So he's finally coming around?"

"Oh yeah. I told you he would. He told me today that I was in a class by myself. I told him I knew he was the man who could make it a class for two."

Bernadette laughed. "I heard that. I'm trying to get Tim to hang out with us, too. It's been way too long since I've had any."

"I heard that!" Cheryl exclaimed.

Lena flushed the toilet and opened the door to her stall to step out.

Cheryl turned toward her and said, "Hey, Lena, what's up?"

"Hi."

Cheryl stood in front of the mirror playing with her hair as she watched Lena washing her hands. Lena purposely did not look in the direction of either woman.

"So, Lena, what do you think of that new guy, Quincy Taylor?" Cheryl asked.

"He's nice," she answered.

"Yeah. He's cute, too, ain't he?"

"I guess so."

"You guess so? Honey, the man is fine! I know you noticed that while you guys were at lunch today. Are you trying to get next to him?" Cheryl asked boldly.

Lena turned to her in shock. "No!"

"No? Well, that's good, 'cause I've got my eye on him. You don't have a problem with that, do you?"

"No. Why would I?"

"Just curious, that's all. I don't wanna be movin' in on anything you've got your eye on. You know us sistahs can't be stabbin' each other in the back," Cheryl said in a matter-of-fact tone.

Lena did not answer. She reached for a paper towel to dry her hands. She was actually quite surprised that Cheryl had even struck up a conversation with her. She had never said more than hello or good-bye to her before. Lena briefly glanced at her reflection in the bathroom mirror and straightened her clothes.

Cheryl looked over at Bernadette and smiled mischievously.

"Honey, you need to loosen up some," Cheryl said to Lena.

Lena looked over at them and just smiled. She turned to the door to leave when Cheryl spoke to her back, "Hey, Lena, have you ever had sex?"

"Cheryl!" Bernadette gasped, looking over at her friend in shock. She could not believe what she had just heard. She knew Cheryl was bold, but to have asked Lena something so personal was way too tactless, even for Cheryl.

"What? I was just wondering," Cheryl said to Bernadette, as though she had every right to ask Lena so private a question.

"That's none of your business!" Bernadette told her.

Lena was just as stunned as Bernadette. Her shock, however, stemmed from an entirely different root. *How could Cheryl know?* Lena wondered. *Is it written all over my face?* She wondered if Quincy could tell, too.

"Good night," Lena said as she quickly exited the bathroom without further responding to Cheryl's rude query.

"Damn, Cheryl, I can't believe you asked her that," Bernadette said with a frown after Lena had left the room.

"What? All she had to do was say yes or no. I know the answer, anyway. She ain't never been with a man."

"What business is it of yours?" Bernadette still wanted to know.

"I just wanted to see what kind of competition I was up against with Quincy. You know you've got to watch out for the quiet ones, Bern. They're usually the biggest freaks. But I ain't worrying about her no more," Cheryl said with a wave of her hand. "That girl ain't never had no man, and as soon as Quincy finds that out he ain't gonna want nothin' else to do with her."

"What makes you think that?"

"Because Quincy's the type of man that ain't got the time to be teaching nobody about what he wants. When he sees that he don't have to play schoolteacher with me, he won't have much time for Little Lena," Cheryl said confidently.

"And what makes you such an expert on what Quincy likes or doesn't like? You don't really know anything about that man," Bernadette said in disgust.

"I've watched him when we're out. Quincy's a lover, not an instructor. He ain't got time for no little girls. He needs a real woman, like me," Cheryl said with confidence as she gazed at herself in the mirror.

ELEVEN

Lena had expected Quincy to come to her sometime before Friday and tell her that he would not be able to see her that evening as they had planned. She expected him to tell her that he would be going out with Cheryl, Reggie, and Bernadette.

"Hey, Lena," Quincy suddenly said over her shoulder, breaking into her reverie. "I haven't seen much of you today. They've kept me pretty busy most of this morning. I didn't even get a chance to go out to lunch," he told her. "Do you mind going to get something to eat before we go to the movies?"

"Oh, you still want to go?"

"Yeah! Don't you?"

"Yes. I just thought you might have changed your mind."

"Why would I do that?" he asked, perplexed.

"Well, I heard Cheryl and Reggie were going dancing. I thought maybe you would rather go with them instead."

He smiled at her and said, "No, thank you. I can only take them in small doses, and I've had my dose for this week. Besides, you and I had already made plans for tonight. Do you think I'd toss aside our plans to go out with them?"

"Well, I know they're your friends and everything," she said shyly.

"They're my coworkers. My friends don't work here. Well, at least most of them," he quickly added.

She smiled up at him, then. Quincy made her feel like no one else ever had. "I don't mind having dinner first," she said softly in answer to his earlier question.

"Good. I'll meet you right here at five, okay?"

"Okay."

He reached across her desk and gently caressed her cheek. "See ya' later, Lena."

"Is there anywhere in particular you'd like to eat?" Quincy asked Lena as they left the bank together.

"No. It doesn't matter."

"What kinds of foods do you like?"

"Most. I'm not very picky. I have a very good appetite."

"Good. You know what I'm in the mood for? Meat and potatoes. I'm starving," Quincy said with a laugh.

"That's right, you didn't eat lunch."

"Nope, I didn't. Listen, I know a great steak house near the movie theater. Would you mind if we went there?"

"No, I don't mind."

He hailed a cab for them, and when one stopped he held the door open for her to get in. The drive, which would have taken about fifteen minutes in normal traffic, took a little over half an hour due to rush hour volume. Quincy didn't seem to mind, though, and Lena was actually quite pleased because it gave her the opportunity to be closer to him than she'd ever been.

When they arrived at the restaurant, the maitre' d escorted them to a cozy table for two. As they moved through the crowded, definitely upscale restaurant to their table, Lena noticed that a majority of the patrons were older white men, a few women, and fewer young people. Everything looked expensive.

When they reached their table, Quincy held Lena's chair as she sat down. A minute after they were seated, they were attended to.

"Good evening. My name is Steven, and I'll be your server tonight. Can I start you off with a cocktail?"

"Lena?"

"I'll just have a Seven-up with a twist of lemon."

"I'll have the same."

As Lena scanned the menu, she noticed that the prices were steep.

"Well, I know what I want. Filet mignon, baked potato, cornbread, and, I guess, a salad," Quincy said right away. "What would you like, Lena?"

"Um, I don't know yet."

"Well, take your time. Every time I come here, I always order the same thing. They have the best filet mignon."

She smiled and said, "I think I'll have the roast chicken." It was one of the least expensive items on the menu.

"Are you sure?" Quincy asked. "I hope you're not ordering that because it's cheap."

Lena quickly responded, "No. I like chicken." She was totally embarrassed.

"Okay."

After their server had come and brought their drinks and taken their food order, Quincy asked, "So, Lena, how long have you been with the bank?"

"Three years."

"Really? You like it there?"

"It's all right. It's an easy job."

"Yeah, I guess."

"I actually started working there while I was going to school, but when my mother got sick I had to drop out so I could take care of her."

"Are you planning to go back?"

"Yes. I plan to register again for the fall semester."

"What school were you attending?"

"Baruch. I was majoring in business administration."

"You have any brothers or sisters?"

"No. I'm an only child."

"I wish," Quincy sighed.

"No you don't. It's too lonely."

"Well, when I was a kid I'd have liked to try it out. I have four sisters, all older than me, so that means I had five mothers growing up." Lena laughed. "And four brothers. I'd really like to have seen what it's like to be an only child."

"Wow, you have a big family," she said with a smile.

"That's an understatement."

"Are your brothers older than you, too?"

"Just one of them."

"Well, at least you always had someone to play with."

"Yeah, and beat up on," he said, with a chuckle. "Where do you live, Lena?"

"In the Bronx."

"Oh. I don't know anything about the Bronx. I grew up in Brooklyn, still live there. I can't seem to get out of there. But I am getting closer to the city."

"I wish I didn't live so far up, but I don't want to sell my parents' house. I grew up there."

"Yeah, I can understand that. So you live there by yourself now?"

"Yes," she said softly.

When they arrived at the movie theater, although they had just finished eating dinner, Quincy asked Lena, "Would you like some popcorn or a soda or anything?"

"No, thank you. I'm gonna run in there, though," she said, and she pointed to the rest room.

"Okay. I'll be right here."

As Lena stood at the sink and washed her hands, she glanced up at her reflection and took a deep breath. Her heart had been beating double time since they left the office. She could not believe she was actually out with him. She smiled at her reflection. She felt good, better than she had in years.

When Lena rejoined him in the lobby, Quincy took her arm and led her to an escalator that would take them to their desired movie.

"Anywhere in particular you'd like to sit?" he asked as he held the door for her.

"No, anywhere you want."

They moved down to about the middle of the theater, and Quincy stepped aside to let her enter the row of seats he selected.

"Do you want to sit on the aisle?" Lena asked.

"No, go all the way in. That way no one has to climb over us."

"Oh, yeah."

Quincy helped her off with her jacket and placed it on the seat next to him before he removed his own and sat down.

"Are you a crier?" he asked suddenly, turning toward her in his seat. "I heard this movie was a real tearjerker."

She smiled and said, "Yes."

"Well, I have a handkerchief here. Just let me know if you need it," he said in a teasing manner.

"Okay, but I do have some tissues."

By the time the credits began to roll at the end of the movie, Lena was, indeed, in tears, but her tears were not caused entirely by the movie they had just watched.

As she sat there with Quincy, enjoying herself in a way she never had before, she had realized all that she had been missing. There had been times when Lena had become frustrated because she felt trapped in the house with her mother. There was no one she could call on to help her. Her father had been an only child, and Sadie's family had fairly disowned her because she had run off and married him when she became pregnant with Lena. Lena felt guilty for a fleeting moment because she was glad that she did not have to be her mother's nursemaid any longer.

"That was a pretty good movie," Quincy said, not yet realizing how much being there had actually affected Lena. When he noticed that she was crying, he put his arm around her and said, "Hey, it was a happy ending."

She was so distraught that for a moment she could not even talk.

"Lena? Lena, what's wrong?" he asked, now very concerned.

"I'm sorry," she moaned. "I'm sorry, Quincy."

"What's the matter, angel? Talk to me. Tell me what's wrong."

"I was just thinking about my mother," she said, sobbing.

"Oh. You miss her a lot, don't you?"

"Yes. But I was just thinking . . . I feel so guilty," Lena groaned.

"Why?"

"Because before my mother died, I never got the chance to go out anywhere. I always had to be home to take care of her. Not that I really had anyplace to go, but now . . . I feel bad because I used to get angry with her because she was sick and I had to take care of her. I'm not happy that she died, but . . . it's like . . ."

Quincy understood right away. "Aw, Lena, don't cry. You don't have anything to feel guilty about. It's only natural that you would want to go out sometimes and be with people your own age. I'm sure your mother understood that, even if you don't. I'm sure if she could see you now she'd be real proud of you, and grateful for the sacrifices you made to be with her. Don't cry, Lena," he said softly as he embraced her. "Come on, don't cry." Quincy removed his handkerchief from his jacket pocket and gently wiped her tears from her face. "Let me see," he said, and he tilted her head up so he could look into her eyes.

He smiled at her. "You're so pretty. Don't be sad. And don't feel guilty. You did everything you could, I'm sure. It's your turn to live. You've got your whole life ahead of you. I'm sure your mother would want you to live it to the fullest."

She tried to catch her breath. "I'm sorry, Quincy. I don't know what came over me," she said with a sigh.

"Stop apologizing. You have nothing to be sorry about."

He held her for a few minutes more until she was calm.

"You okay?" he finally asked.

She nodded.

"You ready to go?"

She nodded again.

He rose from his seat and took her hand and helped her to her feet. Once they were standing, he took her in his arms and hugged her gently.

"You know something, Lena?" he whispered in her ear.

"Huh?"

"You're one in a million."

He leaned back to look into her face and smiled before placing a soft kiss on her fore-head.

"Come on," he said softly. "Let's get out of here."

He helped her on with her jacket and put his arm around her shoulder as they slowly walked up the aisle and out of the theater. Once they were outside, Quincy stepped off the curb to hail a taxi. When one finally stopped after nearly ten minutes, he stepped over and opened the door for Lena.

"Where are we going?" she asked.

"I was going to take you home, unless you want to do something else."

"Oh, no, but I can take the train, Quincy. A cab to the Bronx will be so expensive," she pro-tested.

"No. We won't take the train. We'll take a cab, and don't worry about how much it costs."

"But, Quincy—"

"No buts. And I'm not going to argue with you about it, either."

She looked up at him and was about to say something else when he said, "After you."

Lena got into the cab without further protest. She thought he was too good to be true. He was the type of man she read about in her romance novels.

Once he was in the cab, he asked her, "So where are we going?"

"Laconia Avenue and Two Hundred and twentieth Street. You can take the Major Deegan," Lena said to the driver.

Once they were on their way, Lena turned to Quincy and said, "I'll pay for the cab."

"No, you won't."

"But Quincy—"

"Lena, listen, I'm a bit of a chauvinist. I get insulted when I take a lady out and she doesn't let me pick up the tab. It's an ego thing. You understand."

He smiled at her, and she could not help but smile, too.

"I won't insult you," she said softly.

"Thank you."

"Right here is fine," Lena said to the driver when he pulled up in front of her house.

Quincy paid the driver and got out of the cab, then held out his hand to assist Lena. As the cab pulled away, Quincy opened the gate in Lena's front yard and held it as she passed through it.

"I hope you had a nice time," he said.

She turned toward him and smiled. "I did, Quincy. Thank you."

"It was my pleasure. I hope we can do this again."

She blushed and said, "That would be nice."

They stood there for a moment in awkward silence before Lena asked, "How are you going to get home?"

"I'll take the subway. I just have one question for you, though."

"What's that?"

"How do I get to the subway from here?"

She giggled and pointed toward the far corner. "At the corner, make a right, then walk down two blocks and make a left. It's right there next to the Chinese restaurant."

"Okay. I'll find it."

She smiled shyly and looked up into his eyes and said, "I really had a nice time, Quincy."

"I did too, Lena."

Her hair was pulled back in a ponytail, as usual. As Quincy studied her face, he wondered what she would look like with her long hair free.

"Do you ever wear your hair out?" he asked suddenly.

"Sometimes."

"Can I see?" he asked as he reached behind her to loosen the barrette that held her hair in place. With care, Quincy slowly spread her tresses over her shoulders. He stared at her for a few seconds without saying a word. A warm feeling coursed through his body at the sight of her. "You are so beautiful," he breathed.

"Thank you," she said, and could not help but blush again.

There was an awkward silence again for a few seconds. Lena was hoping that he would kiss her good night, but when he made no move in that direction, she said, "Well, good night."

"Good night, Lena. Have a good weekend," he said with a smile.

"Thank you. You, too."

"Can I have a hug?"

"Yes," she answered immediately.

He put his arms around her and held her close, tenderly. Lena felt as if she had died and gone to heaven. She held him tightly, and as she felt her heart swell with love for him, her eyes began to water. She was so happy; she did not want to move from that spot.

After a few seconds Quincy released her, then took her face gently in his hands and kissed her forehead.

"You know, Lena, I hope that if you ever feel that you need someone to talk to, or someone to just listen, or even a shoulder to cry on, you'll think of me. I'd like to be the person you call on when you just need a friend," Quincy said softly.

Lena melted at his words. Her face was warmed by his caress. "Thank you, I'd like that," she whispered.

They looked into each other's eyes for a few seconds more, and then he kissed her softly on her cheek. "I'll see you Monday, Lena."

She could not speak. She was so overwhelmed with emotion that all she could do was smile.

Quincy started toward the gate. Lena did not move. Once he had stepped through it, he turned back to her and said, "Go on inside. I won't leave until I know you're safely in your house."

Her smile broadened as she turned toward her door. She placed the key in the lock and opened the door slowly.

"Good night, Quincy," she called back to him.

"Good night, Lena."

She closed the door gently, then stood there for a moment hugging herself and smiling brightly. Lena had never felt that way before. It was the most wonderful feeling she had ever had.

On the long subway ride to Brooklyn, Quincy thought of almost nothing but Lena. He was not clear about his feelings for her though. Sometimes he felt an overwhelming need to protect her; she was so vulnerable and naive. At other times, he was so completely turned on by her that all he could think about was making love to her. That feeling had completely overwhelmed him when he had loosened her hair and watched it fall around her beautiful face.

It was so unlike him to fall for someone like her. He was usually put off by bashful women. In the past, he would have never taken the time to try to break through a shy woman's defenses. He was more apt to fall for someone who was much more assertive and confident, like Cheryl, without being pushy.

Suddenly, the memory of her in tears at the end of the movie invaded his mind. He was moved by her feelings of guilt regarding her mother's illness. Quincy could tell that while she was growing up her parents had sheltered her from the world and everything in it. He'd noticed, too, that before the end of the evening she had begun to relax with him. He was glad about that, because he knew how tense she had been when they left work that afternoon, and he wanted her to always be comfortable with him.

Quincy genuinely liked her, too—more than he would have guessed. His thoughts took him back to the way Lena held him when he asked her for a hug. He smiled to himself at the memory. She felt good in his arms, and he could easily imagine himself getting used to holding her that way.

Lena had surprised him, too, when she began grumbling about the cab. He had never met women who complained about being taken home in a cab, no matter how far away from the city they lived—not a single solitary one. He was tickled that she offered to pay for it herself.

Little things like that endeared her to him. One minute she was a bashful young woman, and the next she was offering to pay her own way on their date. She had even offered to pay for the movie.

He loved her smile, and got a kick out of making her blush. Not that it took any great effort; she was one of the most timid women he had ever met. *Damn,* he thought, *I wish I had gotten her number.* He had only given her his business card, which had his home phone number on it. He wanted to kick himself for forgetting to ask for her number. Although he had just left her, he wanted to talk to her again, and he did not want to wait until Monday. He hoped she would use his number and call him on the weekend, but he really did not expect to hear from her. Still, he hoped he would.

When Quincy got off the train in Brooklyn, it was after eleven. He decided to stop by The Underground, a neighborhood bar located a few blocks from where he lived, for a drink. He figured Serge and a couple of his other friends would probably be there.

As soon as he walked in the door of The Underground, he immediately heard someone bellow his name.

"Q.T.! My man! *Whassup?*" One of the fellows he played basketball with on weekends had greeted him in his usual boisterous manner. Quincy knew right away that he had been there for quite some time, and was well on his way to one of his regular binges.

"Yo, what's up, Jerry?" Quincy said with a smile.

The two men slapped palms, and Jerry moved to embrace Quincy.

"Damn, man, how much have you had to drink?" Quincy asked, immediately put off by the smell of Jerry's breath.

"Hey, I been in here since six o'clock. I may be in here till they throw me out!" Jerry said with a slur.

"Well, that will probably be very soon," Quincy said as he moved past Jerry to greet his best friend.

"What's up, man?"

"Hey, Serge, what's happenin'?" Quincy said. He greeted his buddy with a soulful handshake.

"Ain't nothin', man. Where you been? I've been trying to call you."

"I went to the movies."

"Who with?"

Quincy smiled at him and said, "You don't know her."

"Yeah, so? Who'd you go with?"

"Someone from my office."

"That babe Cheryl you were telling me about?"

"Hell, no!"

"Then who?"

"Lena. The receptionist in my department."

"Is that the one you were telling me about that's real shy?" Serge looked at Quincy with a smirk. "So what are you trying to do, bring her out of her shell?"

"Forget you, man."

Serge laughed.

He was taller than Quincy by about three inches, and much thinner. Serge was clean-shaven with a dark brown complexion, and he had short, straight, black hair, dark brown eyes, a small pointed nose, and relatively thin lips. He and Quincy became friends when they were in junior high school, soon after Serge and his family moved to the United States from Kingston, Jamaica. He looked much younger than his thirty-three years. When he and Quincy went out together, Serge often had to show identification before he was admitted to a club or permitted to buy a drink in a bar.

"Hey, you know who's here looking for you?" Serge asked with a wicked grin.

"Who?"

At that moment, someone pinched Quincy on

his backside. He turned sharply and was surprised to see his friend, Mayella, standing there.

"Hi, honey," she said flirtatiously.

"Hey, what's up, May? How you doin'?" Quincy bent and kissed her cheek. "How long you been here?"

"Since about ten-thirty. I was hoping you would stop in."

"Did you come in here looking for me?"

"Can you think of any other reason I would come into this dive?" she said with a grin.

Quincy just laughed.

"What are you drinking?" he asked her.

"Bacardi and Coke."

"Do you have a table?" Quincy asked, gesturing toward the back of the club.

"Yeah. I'm with couple of my girlfriends."

"Go back to your table. I'll bring it to you."

"All right."

When she walked away, Quincy turned to Serge and sighed.

"What's the matter?"

"I don't feel like being bothered with May tonight."

He leaned over the bar and ordered her drink.

"You drinkin' rum tonight?" Serge asked, knowing that Quincy usually did not drink anything but beer.

"Nah, that's for May."

"You not drinkin'?"

"Nah. I'm not gonna stay."

"What's the matter?" Serge asked again, immediately recognizing that his friend seemed to be quite preoccupied.

"Nothing. I've just got a lot of stuff on my mind, that's all."

Quincy was sorry he had not gone straight home. He did not mind that Serge was questioning him about what was on his mind, or even that he teased him about his date with Lena. The Underground was just too damn noisy for him. And then there was Mayella. After being with Lena, he felt as though he would be slapping her in the face if he took Mayella home tonight. Besides, he did not want to be with Mayella. He wanted to get to know more about Lena.

The bartender placed the drink he ordered for Mayella on the bar, and Quincy paid for it. "Keep the change."

He immediately headed back to where Mayella was sitting with two of her friends.

"Hi, Quincy," one of them called cheerfully.

"Hey, Judy, Shelly. How y'all doin'?"

He placed Mayella's drink on the table in front of her.

"Thanks, Quincy."

She was sitting on the aisle, so he squatted down next to her chair and whispered in her ear, "I'm not gonna hang out tonight."

"You goin' home?"

"Yeah."

"You want me to come with you?"

"Not tonight, baby. I've got a lot stuff on my mind right now. I wouldn't be much company to you," he said honestly.

"You wanna talk?"

He smiled at her, but said, "Nah. I'm just gonna go home and hit the sack. I'm kinda tired."

"All right. You okay?" she asked with genuine concern.

"Yeah." He sighed. "I'm just tired."

"Call me?"

"I will." He kissed her softly on the cheek, then said, "I'll see you later."

When he stood back up, he removed a twenty-dollar bill from his pocket and said, "Buy yourself a couple of drinks on me."

"Thanks, Quincy."

He walked back up to the bar to rejoin Serge. He held out his hand to slap Serge five as he said, "Yo, man, I'ma cut out."

"Hey, you all right?"

"Yeah."

"You think you gonna feel like playing some ball tomorrow?" Serge asked.

"About what time?"

"Probably about eleven."

"Yeah, give me a call. I'll play."

"All right, man. Take it easy."

"Yeah. Later," Quincy said as he headed for the door.

As he leisurely strolled home, all he could think about was Lena. He wanted to be with her. That was all he wanted.

TWELVE

Lena did not really do anything all weekend other than grocery shop. She walked around in a state of euphoria. By Sunday, she had replayed the events of Friday evening in her mind at least a hundred times.

She had never known anyone like Quincy.

During the time when she attended church regularly, she had been approached a few times by young men who also attended the church. She was always too shy to really talk with any of them though, and they had never made any real attempts to make her feel at ease. When she stopped going to church, the little bit of male attention she had received stopped, too.

She wondered if Quincy felt the way she did, or if he was just trying to be a friend. After all, he had said he wanted her to feel as though she could call on him if she ever felt she needed to talk to someone. The more she thought about it, she figured that was probably the extent of it. He just wanted to be her friend. *He probably has a girlfriend,* she thought. Someone as handsome and as sweet as he was had to have a girlfriend somewhere, she reasoned. *It really doesn't make sense to get my hopes up,* she thought.

She took the business card Quincy had given her out of her pocketbook. She wanted to call him at home, but did not have the courage to dial the number. *What if he's with someone when I call?* That would be devastating.

Lena walked into to her bedroom and over to the mirror on the dresser. She carefully studied her reflection. *He told me I was beautiful.* Lena had always thought her looks were rather plain. She thought her eyes were too small, and her nose too flat. She picked up her brush from the dresser and began to brush her hair. She hardly ever wore it out. When Quincy took it out of the barrette the other evening, Lena had been so embarrassed by his attention that she could not even speak. He liked it out, though. She decided to put her hair in rollers and wear it out tomorrow when she went to work—just for him.

Quincy stayed home all day Sunday. He had hoped Lena would call. He could not get her out of his mind, no matter how he tried. She seemed to invade every thought he had.

He tried to watch a basketball game on television that afternoon, but found himself daydreaming about her. He had already decided that the first thing he would do when he went to work the next day was try to talk her into having lunch with him.

On Monday morning Quincy rose early, and after showering he put on his navy-blue pinstripe suit. He was always complimented on how

sharp he looked when he wore the suit, and he
wanted to look his best when he saw Lena. He
doused himself in Calvin Klein's Eternity for
Men, and hoped Lena would like it as much as
he did.

When Quincy arrived at the office that morning, he was pleasantly surprised to see that Lena
had curled her hair and was wearing it out. She
was speaking with a visitor to the bank, so he
could not tell her how beautiful he thought she
looked, though he wanted to. When she noticed
him, though, she smiled at him. Quincy returned her smile and winked at her.

A half-hour later, Quincy got up from his
desk, put his suit jacket back on, and went to
talk to Lena.

"Good morning, Quincy," Maritza said as he
stepped out of his office. She had not been at
her desk when he arrived.

"Good morning, Maritza. How was your weekend?"

"It was great. How was yours?"

"Pretty good, thanks. I'll be back in a couple
of minutes."

"All right. That's a nice suit you're wearing,"
she told him as he walked away.

He turned back to her and smiled. "Thanks."

When he stepped into the reception area,
Lena was on the telephone. She did not see him
approach.

"Okay, I'll give him the message," she said
into the receiver. "Good-bye."

"Good morning."

Turning at the sound of his voice, she smiled brightly and said, "Good morning, Quincy."

"Your hair looks great."

"Thank you," she said with a blush.

"You're welcome. How was the rest of your weekend?"

"It was nice, thank you. How was yours?"

"Well, it was all downhill after Friday. I couldn't find anything to do that was as exciting as spending the evening with you."

She just grinned.

"What are you doing for lunch today?"

"Nothing special."

"Did you bring lunch from home?"

"No, not today."

"Good. Would you have lunch with me?"

"Yes."

"I really like your hair like that."

"Thank you, Quincy. I figured it was time for a change."

"Well, it's a definite change for the better."

"Thank you. I really like your suit, too," Lena said. She could not believe she had actually said that.

Quincy was surprised, too, pleasantly so. "Thank you, Lena. I was hoping you'd like it," he said truthfully.

"So, I'll meet you here at one?" he asked.

"Okay."

THIRTEEN

By Wednesday Lena and Quincy had eaten lunch together every day. Quincy found that the more time he spent with her, the more time he wanted to spend with her. He noticed that she was much more relaxed with him now, and he was happy about that.

When they returned from lunch that day, Cheryl and Reggie were standing near the elevator talking. Cheryl looked at Lena with a cynical smile, but did not address her. She said, "Quincy, what are you doing this Friday?"

Lena noticed immediately that her question was directed at Quincy and Quincy alone, so she continued to walk to her desk to relieve the person who had covered for her while she was at lunch.

Quincy paused to answer. "Nothing, why?"

"I'm having a birthday party Friday night. I'd be very disappointed if you didn't come." Cheryl grabbed his arm and tried to cuddle up to him.

Lena noticed the way Cheryl was holding on to Quincy, and she felt a twinge of jealousy and insecurity.

Being facetious, Quincy answered, "Well,

Lord knows I wouldn't want to disappoint you, Cheryl."

"I would hope not. Here's my address," she said, as she handed him an invitation. "We'll be starting at around ten o'clock. I want to see your face in the place."

"All right, I'll try to make it," he lied. He had no intention of going anywhere near Cheryl's house.

Quincy really disliked the way she had purposely excluded Lena. He walked away from them, and as he passed through the reception area he stopped at Lena's desk.

"Cheryl's having a birthday party Friday night," he said, showing her the invitation.

"Oh, that should be nice," Lena said with absolutely no enthusiasm.

"What are you doing Friday?" Quincy asked her.

"Nothing."

"You wanna go to the movies again?"

Lena looked up at him in surprise. "Aren't you going to Cheryl's party?"

"No."

"But—"

"But, what?"

"I think she likes you," Lena said. She turned her face away from him and started shuffling papers on her desk.

Quincy stared down at her. "Yeah, so?"

"She'll probably be upset if you don't go," she said, and still would not look at him.

"Yeah, so?" he repeated as he continued to stare at her.

She looked up at him. "Wouldn't you rather go out with them?"

"No. I'd rather go out with you. That's why I asked *you* if *you* wanted to go to the movies."

She could not help but smile, then. "What do you want to see?"

"Whatever. It doesn't matter."

He acted as though there had been no mention of Cheryl or her party.

"Okay. Do you want to go straight from work again?"

"Yeah. We can get something to eat first."

"All right, but this time, I'll treat," Lena insisted.

"Now, we're not going to go through that again, I hope," he said with a chuckle.

She laughed.

Maritza came through the reception area at that moment.

"Oh, hi, Quincy. I left two messages on your desk. I'll be right back," she said. "How you doin', Lena?" she asked.

"I'm fine, Maritza. How are you?"

"Fine, thanks."

"Well, let me get back to work. I'll talk to you later, okay?" Quincy said to Lena.

"Okay. Bye."

He winked at her before he walked off.

Later that afternoon, an outside messenger stepped off the elevator carrying a bouquet of flowers. He stepped up to the reception desk and asked, "Do you have someone by the name of Lena Caldwell here?"

"I'm Lena Caldwell."

"Well then, these are for you. Could you sign next to the X, please?"

He handed her a clipboard with a checklist attached. Perplexed, she signed the sheet and handed the board back to him. He handed her the flowers, said, "Have a nice day," then turned and walked back to the elevator bank.

"Thank you. You, too," Lena replied, then quickly dismissed him from her mind to examine the beautiful bouquet in front of her. It was an assortment of roses, carnations, daisies, lilies, and a few others she could not name. They were breathtaking, and their sweet fragrance filled the air.

As she was unwrapping them, Maritza was passing by her desk. "Oh, what beautiful flowers."

"Aren't they?" Lena agreed.

"Are they from your boyfriend?" Maritza asked when she stopped to admire the bouquet more closely.

"No. I don't have a boyfriend."

"Is it your birthday?"

"No."

"Well, who are they from?" Maritza asked, as curious as Lena.

"I don't know. I haven't even looked at the card."

Lena pulled off the tiny envelope stapled to the cellophane wrapper and opened it with trembling fingers. She pulled the card out and read the message written there. *"You are truly one in a million. Q."*

Lena smiled brightly, and her eyes began to water. She shook her head in amazement.

"Who are they from?"

"A friend of mine," she said with a grin.

"Must be a special friend," Maritza said with a knowing smile.

Lena nodded. "Yes, very special."

"Well, they're beautiful flowers, Lena. Enjoy them."

"Thank you, Maritza."

Once Maritza was gone, Lena reread the card that came with the bouquet. *He thinks I'm one in a million.* Her heart was so full of love for him at that moment that she felt as if it would burst. She picked up the telephone and dialed his extension.

"Quincy Taylor speaking."

"Thank you, Quincy," she said softly.

He smiled at hearing her voice. "You got them already?"

"Yes, and they're beautiful."

"Well, I'm glad you're enjoying them."

"I am. Thank you."

"You're welcome, Lena. That's just a little something to show my appreciation."

"For what?"

"Well, just for being the special person that you are, that's all."

"I think you're pretty special, too, Quincy."

"Thank you, Lena."

Quincy had turned his back to the door and was absently gazing out the window as he spoke to Lena, so he had not seen or heard Maritza enter his office.

"You should come out and see them when you get a chance," Lena suggested.

"I will. I'll be out in about ten minutes."

"Okay."

"See ya."

When he turned back around to hang up the phone, Maritza was standing there with a big smile on her face.

"What?"

"You sent her those flowers?"

"Were you eavesdropping?" he asked, grinning.

"No. I came in here to ask you about these folders you put on my desk, but I overheard part of your conversation."

"I'm not big on office gossip," he told her.

"Neither am I. From your lips to my ears, it won't go any further than that. I swear."

He looked at her without any further comment.

She smiled knowingly.

"They're really beautiful, Quincy. That was real sweet of you."

"Well, that's just the kind of guy I am. Now, what was it you wanted to ask me?"

FOURTEEN

Friday was April twenty-third. The temperature was expected to go up to almost eighty degrees. The sun was out, the sky was a beautiful shade of blue, and there was not a cloud to be seen.

Lena had dressed for the weather. She wore a teal-blue linen pantsuit that she had designed and tailored herself. Under the jacket she wore a teal-blue and gold brocade vest over a fuscia silk T-shirt.

When Quincy arrived at the office that morning he greeted her enthusiastically.

"Good morning, gorgeous!" Normally, he would not have addressed her in that manner at the office, but they were alone in the reception area.

"Good morning, Quincy. How are you?"

"Great! How're you doin'?"

"I'm fine."

"Yes, you most certainly are."

Lena blushed and said, "You flatter me too much."

"Nothing you don't deserve," he told her.

That afternoon, however around three o'clock, Quincy came out to Lena's desk.

"Hey, Lena, there's been a change in plans," he said.

Immediately, as if a helium balloon had been released into the atmosphere, a memory rose to the surface, and she recalled that Cheryl was having a birthday party that evening. She automatically assumed that he had changed his mind and wanted to go.

"Oh. You can't go tonight?" she asked in a somber tone.

"Oh, yeah! We're still on. I was just thinking that instead of going to the movies, since it's so nice outside . . . what do you think about going to an amusement park?"

She looked up at him, and a smile formed on her lips. *An amusement park*, she thought. *That's original.* "I haven't been to an amusement park in . . . oh my goodness, I can't even remember when," she said.

"So, let's do it! You're wearing slacks and I can just pull off my tie and get loose. How 'bout it?"

"All right. Where do you wanna go?"

"Let's go to Great Adventure."

"All right."

"I drove in this morning, so we can pick up the car, grab something to eat on the way, and just go," Quincy told her.

"Okay. That sounds like fun."

"Yeah, I thought so. I figured we could do something a little different. It's too nice out to be stuck inside."

"You're right about that. Okay, so we'll go to Great Adventure."

When they left the office that evening, Quincy and Lena stopped at a fast food restaurant and picked up burgers and fries, which they ate during the drive to New Jersey. By the time they reached their destination it was seven twenty-five. They were not surprised to see that the park was very crowded. The weather had held up, and the night was very warm.

"Are you still hungry?" Quincy asked Lena after paying their admission.

"Oh, no. I'm fine."

"Okay, then, let's go get on the roller coaster," Quincy said, taking her hand and pulling her in that direction.

"The roller coaster?" she said, pulling back. "I've never been on one before."

"You're kidding. Aw, come on, Lena. They're fun. How can you go to an amusement park and not get on the roller coaster?"

"I've done it plenty of times."

"Come on. You'll love it. I guarantee it."

"I don't know, Quincy," she hedged.

"Come on," he whined. "Please? Pretty please?"

He pushed out his lips like a little boy and made a face that she thought was so funny she could not help laughing. He had to laugh himself. When they had both calmed down, Quincy continued with his gentle persuasion.

"Seriously, Lena. Come with me. I promise you'll enjoy it. I don't want to go on without you."

"Oh, Quincy—"

"Please, Lena?"

"All right," she said, nervously giving in.

Quincy was excited that she had decided to get on the ride with him.

When they reached the boarding platform, he pulled Lena toward the first car.

"Not the first car, Quincy!" Lena said as she pulled back.

"That's the only way to ride it, baby."

Lena did not know why she had let him talk her into getting on. She was petrified. She got in the car, and he fastened them in. He put his arm around her shoulder to comfort her, because he could see she was very nervous. He kissed her on the side of her head.

"Don't worry, angel. You're gonna love it."

"I hope so."

When the ride slowly started, Lena let out a yelp. Her stomach knotted up as the train slowly climbed the track. She grabbed Quincy's arm and squeezed it tightly.

When the train reached the peak of the ride, it seemed to pause for a second or two before it began its dip. Lena made the mistake of looking down. As it started its descent in the next second, Lena screamed at the top of her lungs.

By the time the roller coaster had run its course and they were getting off, Lena was wild with glee. "That was great!" she yelled. "I loved that!"

Quincy was very pleased. "I knew you would."

"I really did, Quincy. That was a lot of fun. I was always too scared to get on a roller coaster before."

"I told you it was nothing."

As they were walking away from the ride, Lena suddenly stopped in her tracks. She looked at Quincy in a strange manner.

"What?" he asked.

She smiled impishly and asked, "Can we go on again?"

"Uh-oh. I think I've created a monster," Quincy joked.

They rode the roller coaster two more times before Lena was satisfied. After that, they got on a number of other rides, most of which Lena would never have ventured to get on before. She was having the time of her life.

After they'd had their fill of the rides, they decided to visit a video arcade room. Lena headed directly for a space invader game as she dug in her pockets looking for change.

"You wanna play?" she asked him with a mischievous smile.

"Sure, I'll play."

She put four quarters in the machine and started right up.

Quincy watched her intently as she played the video game with an enthusiasm he had never seen in her before. She was fascinated. Her beautiful face took on a whole new look in light of her happiness. He noticed, too, that she was quite skilled.

"Where'd you learn to play like that?" he suddenly asked her.

"At school," she answered without taking her eyes off the screen.

He decided not to bother her and just let her play, which she did for quite a time. When she finally relinquished the controls, she stepped away from the machine with a satisfied smile.

"You're pretty good at this. I don't know if I want to play you," Quincy joked as he stepped up to the game for his turn.

Almost twenty minutes later, she stepped away from the machine for the final time in triumph, after soundly beating him.

Quincy pretended to be insulted. "All right. You got that. But how good are you at skeeball?" Quincy asked with a smug smile.

They stayed in the arcade playing video games for over an hour. When they finally left, Quincy asked, "Are you hungry?"

"Yes."

"Me, too. Where do you want to eat?"

"I think I saw a few places near the Ferris wheel."

"Okay, let's go over there."

As they walked toward the food court Quincy put his arm around Lena's shoulder, and she put her arm around his waist. They were passing one of the carnival games when Lena stopped and cried, "Ooh, Quincy, are you any good at the water pistol race?"

"Hmph," he grunted. "I'm a crack shot."

"I'll race you," she challenged.

"Are you sure you want to do this?" he asked teasingly.

"Positive."

They stepped over to the game stand and bought two chances. There were eight other people racing, too. When the hawker rang the bell to start the race, Lena took aim and fired, concentrating with all her might.

A minute later Lena cried, "I won!"

Quincy was tickled that she was so skilled at all of the games they had played that day. He was tickled, too, at seeing this side of her. The shy little woman that was Lena Caldwell when they first met was nowhere to be found.

She was awarded a small stuffed animal.

"You wanna play again?" she suddenly asked Quincy.

"Again?"

"Yeah, so I can get the big bear," she said, pointing up to the rack that held the prizes.

There was a big white teddy bear with a red bow around its neck and a big red heart in the center of its chest. She did not tell Quincy, but she wanted to win the bear so she could give it to him.

He agreed to race her again. She won. Again.

With this victory, she was able to trade her small toy for a bigger one. But she still had her mind set on getting the big white bear.

She challenged him to another game, but he declined.

Two couples had stepped near the stand, and Lena called out to them. "Would y'all like to play?"

After a moment's hesitation they decided to play, so she challenged all four of them.

She won a third time.

The two men who were playing challenged her again because their egos were bruised by the loss to Lena. Several other people bought chances, too, and that increased the odds against her. But she already knew that if she could win this game she would get the white bear. She readily accepted the challenge. She picked up her pistol and aimed at the bull's-eye centered in the clown's mouth in front of her and awaited the hawker's bell. Less than a minute after the bell sounded, Lena had won her fourth game in a row.

She jumped with glee and cried, "I want that big white bear!" She snatched the stuffed animal Quincy was holding from his hands and handed it back to the hawker.

When the man reached up and brought down the bear for her, she hugged it as if she were a small child.

"This was always my favorite game at the amusement park," she told Quincy happily.

"I can tell," he said, as they started on their way.

"I remember the first time I won at that game. I was at Coney Island with my father. I was a kid. I just got this funny looking mug, but I was so happy."

Quincy chuckled. He loved seeing her excited this way.

While they grabbed a bite to eat in one of the many eateries in the park Lena opened up to Quincy about her childhood, and life. Quincy hung on her every word, because this was the most he had ever heard her talk about herself.

He was not surprised to learn that her parents had made it their business to keep Lena close to home in their effort to protect her from all of the terrible things that went on in their neighborhood and the world. She attended a private elementary school, which her mother or father drove her to and from every day. She was never allowed to participate in any after school activities, so she was never really given the opportunity to make friends. When she started high school, she became somewhat of an outcast because she was forbidden to take part in any of the school's functions or clubs—hence, her shyness.

Once she had graduated from high school and begun attending college part-time she tried to make friends, but found that she was not very good at it, so she opted for reclusion. She wanted to tell him how much his friendship meant to her, but regardless of how much more comfortable she felt with him, she did not have the courage.

After their meal, they strolled casually around the park until Quincy noticed that Lena had yawned a few times.

"Are you tired?" he asked.

It was almost midnight.

"Yes, I am," she said as she tried to stifle yet another yawn.

"Come on, let's go home."

As they walked slowly toward the parking lot, Lena held tightly to Quincy's arm. When they reached his car, Lena handed the teddy bear she had won to Quincy. "I want you to have this," she said softly. "Because . . ." She blushed and lowered her head for a moment before she sighed and continued. "Because you're special."

Quincy took the bear and smiled at her, although he did not respond right away. He was actually a little embarrassed. "No one's ever given me a teddy bear before," he finally said. "Thank you, Lena. I think you're pretty special, too."

They stood together in silence for a few seconds before Lena said, "I can't remember the last time I had this much fun. Thank you, Quincy. I really had a great time tonight."

"I'm glad you did, Lena. I did, too. I'm glad I was able to talk you into getting on the roller coaster. And by the way, I happened to noticed that quite a change came over you once we got off," he said with a smirk.

She started to giggle. "I know. That was so much fun, though. I didn't know it was going to be."

Quincy smiled at her lovingly as he reached for her hand and gently squeezed it. "I'm really happy that you had so much fun today. We've gotta do this again."

"I know. When?"

They both laughed.

Quincy released her hand and stepped away from her for a moment to unlock the car door. He opened the back door, set the teddy bear on the seat, then fastened the seat belt around it.

"I don't want him falling all over the place," he said to Lena, explaining his actions.

She just grinned at him.

He then unlocked the passenger door for her.

He looked over at her as he slowly opened it for her. She was about to step into the car when he suddenly grabbed her, halting her movement. When she turned to him, he pulled her into his arms and kissed her lips.

Lena was stunned at first, and her eyes widened in reaction to his aggressiveness. But she quickly relaxed and melted against him. When their lips parted, Lena looked up at him in a daze. She had never been kissed that way before. Quincy, too, was in a bit of a daze. He had not realized until then just how much he really cared for her.

His embrace became more tender, and he placed his lips on hers for another kiss, this time parting her lips with his tongue. Lena placed her arms around him, squeezing him with all her might. This was the moment she had waited for all her life. On many occasions, Lena had dreamt about Quincy holding her in his arms and kissing her this way, so many times that the reality of it was staggering. She did not want to let him go.

Although it was dark and there were people moving about in the parking lot, Lena was oblivious to them. In the past, she would have been horrified at the thought of anyone witnessing her in this light, but now she did not care. She was in love with Quincy, and from the way he held her Lena gleaned that he cared about her just as much.

When their lips finally parted they stood in each other's arms for a moment, relishing the feel of their bodies pressed close together. She could tell how excited he was, for his body revealed it. Lena had never felt anything like it before, and could not disguise her own excitement at feeling him that way.

"You are so beautiful, Lena," he whispered as he gazed into her eyes.

As she looked up into his beautiful brown eyes, she wanted to tell him how much she loved him, but she held her tongue for fear that he might think she was pushing him too fast.

After a time, he reluctantly released her. He sighed and said, "I guess we'd better head on back."

She did not speak. Lena stepped into the car and sat down as he closed the door for her. As he walked around the front of the car to the driver's side, he looked through the windshield at her with a combination of reverence, confusion, and desire.

Once he was behind the wheel of the car, Quincy put the key in the ignition and started the car without a word. He reached over and turned on the tape deck. The soft relaxing music of Gerald Albright flowed from the speakers. Lena sat with her hands in her lap, looking straight ahead for fear that he would be able to read her thoughts. Feelings and impulses were going through her body like nothing she had ever experienced. She had felt a tingling in her loins when he pressed himself against her. The only other thing that had ever triggered such a reaction was a steamy scene in one of her romance novels. Suddenly, he reached over and took her hand. She looked over at him then, and smiled when she saw his smile.

"You're really something, you know," he said softly.

"So are you."

They began their journey to Lena's home without another word between them. For most of the ride they simply enjoyed each other, not feeling the need to talk. When they were halfway through their trip, Lena dozed off. The traffic was moderately heavy, although by this time it was well past midnight. Many times while she slept, as he sat behind the wheel of his car waiting for the traffic to flow, Quincy gazed over at her, captivated by the beauty of her, inside and out.

He genuinely cared for her, but aside from that Quincy wanted to make love to her. The thought of holding Lena's naked body in his arms occupied his mind for most of the ride. He nursed a very uncomfortable erection as a result, but he could not suppress the thought. He did not want to take her home. He did not want to leave her. Quincy wanted to be able to hold her in his arms for the rest of the night and all of the next day and the next.

She was curled up in the seat with her head laying on the headrest, facing him. Her legs were tucked underneath her. As Quincy studied the sleeping beauty, he realized that he had fallen in love with her. Of all the women he had known in his life, of all the women he had loved or lusted after, he had never felt for any of them they way he did about Lena. He felt a need to

be with her, to protect her, and to allow her to
be the warm and gentle soul that she was. He
had found, to his delight, that she was not a
loner by choice. She was, in fact, a free spirit
who needed a reason—or more aptly, an opportunity—to let her spirit soar.

Despite the fact that he had only been to
Lena's house once, Quincy had no trouble lo-
cating it once they got off the highway. He
pulled up in front of her house and parked in
her driveway, but did not wake her right away.
He sat there and gazed at her longingly for almost five minutes before he woke her up.

"Lena. Lena," he said softly when he gently
shook her awake. "We're here, sweetheart."

Lena came out of her sleep slowly and
stretched and yawned. "We're home already?"

"Yeah. We're home."

"You didn't have any problems getting here?"
she asked sleepily.

"Not a one."

She sighed and said, "I'm sorry for falling
asleep on you, Quincy."

"That's all right. Don't worry about it."

He leaned over and kissed her softly on her
lips, then opened his door to get out of the car.
He walked around to Lena's door to help her
out of the car.

She seemingly collapsed in his arms when she
stood up. Quincy caught her and held her close
to him.

"Lucky for me you're a good catch," Lena
said, not realizing the significance of her double
entendre.

"I like to think so," he said, teasing her.

Lena stood on her own, then. She looked up into his eyes and asked, "You're going to come inside, right?"

Quincy stared at her for a few seconds before he answered. *If I asked her to make love, she probably would,* he thought. Although what he felt in his heart for Lena was very real, Quincy knew he would hurt her if he let his desire dictate his actions. "No. I'm going to go on home and let you get some rest. But I'll call you tomorrow, okay?"

Lena was disappointed, and it showed. "Oh . . . okay."

Quincy immediately took her in his arms. He whispered, "I care about you, Lena. More than I can tell you. We've got plenty of time." Quincy leaned back to look into her eyes. They were filled with tears. "I don't ever want to hurt you. You're very important to me." He kissed her lips softly. "Get some sleep, angel. I'll talk to you tomorrow."

Lena turned away from him and walked to her front door. She was angry and hurt, and she felt rejected.

"Lena."

She had the key in the lock and was about to turn it when she looked back at him. As he gazed into her tear-filled eyes, Quincy yearned to tell her the true extent of what he felt for her, but he knew he had to take his time. "Good night."

"Good night," she murmured. Then she

turned the key, opened the door, and went inside.

Quincy stood looking at her front door for a few seconds before he moved back to his car. *You did the right thing*, he told himself. *Mama would be proud.* But, oh, how he wanted her. The mere thought of Lena gave him an erection. There was more to it than that. His heart was in on all this. To Quincy, Lena was a goddess. He did not feel worthy of her. Quincy was no Goody Two-shoes by any stretch of the imagination. He was a healthy, red-blooded, African-American bachelor, and he loved his life. He was not looking to make any changes, and he was not quite ready to settle down. But he would never play Lena. Not in a million years. She was too important.

Quincy pondered his situation all the way home. When he awoke Saturday morning, his first thought was of Lena. "Oh, girl, what are you doing to me?" he said.

He called her at noon.

Lena had waited all morning for his call. After his rejection of her last night, she had not been certain he would.

"Good afternoon, angel," Quincy said tenderly when she answered the phone.

"Hi, Quincy."

"And how are you this fine afternoon?"

"I'm okay. How are you?"

"I'm doing great. I just got in from playing ball with Serge. I was about to jump in the shower, but I wanted to check in with you first, before you go out."

"I'm not going anywhere today," Lena said solemnly.

"You're not? Good. Think you'd feel like seeing a movie with Serge and Karen?"

"Is that his girlfriend?"

"Yeah, and I'd really like you two to meet. She's really good people, and I think you'll like her a lot. I figure since you're going to be seeing so much of each other, you might as well get to know each other."

"Why do you say that?"

"Why do I say what?"

"That we'll be seeing so much of each other?" Lena asked.

"Because you will. Serge is my main man, and wherever Serge goes, Karen goes. Practically. We're all very close, angel, and since we'll be spending so much time together—" Quincy realized what he was saying, and slowed himself down. "I mean, if you want to hang out with us. I shouldn't just assume you want to be with me. I'm sorry."

"No, Quincy, I do," Lena answered hurriedly, then realized how desperate she must sound to him. "I mean, if you want me to."

His tone softened. "I've never wanted anything so much in my life, Lena."

"Me, too," she responded softly.

A feeling of warmth spread through his body at the sound of her voice, and the words "I love you" were on Quincy's tongue, but he bit them back. She was too vulnerable, and he had to be sure. To lighten the mood, Quincy said, "Listen,

I'm going to jump in the shower real quick.
Then I'll come and get you, okay?"

"Okay."

"I'll call you when I'm getting ready to walk
out the door. See you later, angel."

"Bye."

Quincy took a deep breath when he hung up
the phone. *Chill out, man. You almost lost it there
for a moment.* He had never been one to let his
guard down so quickly, but Lena made him feel
as if he could tell her anything that was on his
mind. Suddenly, his thoughts returned to last
night, when he had kissed her for the first time.
She had been shocked, and he felt her initial
resistance. But when she relaxed in his arms and
began to return his kiss, his heart leapt. She was
a great kisser, and because he was already
turned on by being with her, the kiss had just
caused his heartbeat to accelerate even more.

A voice in his head repeated what he'd
thought all night and most of the day: *She's the
one, Quincy.* All he had to do was accept it.

Lena's melancholy mood lightened immediately when Quincy said they would be spending
a lot of time together. After last night she had
not been certain where their relationship would
go. She had slept fitfully all night because she
thought he was not serious about them. *But he
wants me to meet his friends.* That was a good sign,
she figured. Lena wanted to know everything
about him and be a part of everything that was
important to him. She wanted to meet his parents, and his sisters and brothers, too. The fact
that he wanted her to get to know Serge's girl-

friend meant he wanted her in his life, too. She was overjoyed.

Quincy arrived at Lena's house at a few minutes past two. Since they had never been out together on the weekend, and Lena was used to seeing him dressed in business attire, she was surprised when she opened the door and saw him dressed in jeans and sneakers. His incredible torso was outlined clearly by the body-hugging T-shirt he wore, and Lena had to catch her breath at the sight of him.

"Hi, angel," Quincy said. Then, without hesitation, he stepped into the house and kissed Lena softly on the mouth.

A dreamy, "Hi," was all she could manage.

She closed the door, and before she had let go of the doorknob Quincy had taken her in his arms. "You still mad at me?"

Lena was puzzled. "Mad about what?"

"Because I opted to go home last night."

She was embarrassed. She hadn't realized that he'd noticed her change of mood.

"I—"

"Believe me, Lena, it wasn't because I didn't want to stay. I really did, but . . . well, I don't know whether I could have remained a gentleman last night. See, I was feeling quite . . . amorous, and I didn't want to rush into anything and have you regret it later."

"Why are you so sure I'd regret it later?"

"I'm not, but I . . . I care about you so much, Lena, that I just want to make sure I do everything right, and that means using my head to make decisions, and not my body."

Lena looked into his eyes and smiled. "Thank you for caring."

He kissed her softly. "Thank you for being you."

Their lips came together again, this time in a slow sensuous kiss, their tongues wrestling gently. Quincy's arms tightened around Lena's waist, and soon she was off her feet. Quincy held her as close as he could while exploring the inside of her mouth with his tongue. Lena loved the way he kissed her, and she could feel, once again, how excited he was by their intimacy.

Their lips parted, and Quincy eased her back to the floor. "See, there I go again. We'd better leave before I lose my mind."

Lena just chuckled.

The drive to Karen's apartment in Harlem took about forty-five minutes. Quincy gave Lena the rundown on how Karen and Serge met.

Karen had been a blind date for Quincy, set up by a friend of his. Quincy explained that his first thought upon seeing Karen in person was of Serge, and how similar they were in appearance. It was not so much that she looked like him, but her physique and mannerisms reminded him of his friend. He had taken her to a soul food restaurant not far from where she lived, and from the first minutes of their conversation Quincy had known there was no love connection. As the evening wore on, however, her similarity to Serge became more prominent. Before they finished eating dinner, they acknowledged that there could be nothing between them, but Quincy could not resist telling Karen about how much she reminded him of his best friend. He happened to have a picture of Serge in his car. Earlier in the day, he had picked up the photos he had taken when he and Serge were on vacation in Jamaica and visiting Serge's family. Karen liked his looks right off, so Quincy offered to introduce her. She accepted.

It so happened that Quincy had planned to go to Serge's apartment that night after his dinner date. He promised Karen that if she came with him and she did not like Serge, he would see her home.

Normally, Karen would not have ventured so far away from home with a man she barely knew. She had sensed Quincy's sincerity from the start, however, and although she knew he was not the man for her, she felt as though she could trust him not to deceive her. She went with him to Serge's place.

Serge was completely unaware of what was happening with Quincy and Karen when they arrived at his apartment that night. Quincy had suggested calling ahead and bringing him up to speed, but Karen thought she would get a truer picture of the man if he was not trying to impress her.

They ended up hanging out for the rest of the night. The rapport between the three of them was easy and automatic. They went to a movie, then stopped in at a nearby nightclub and had a couple of drinks. When Karen excused herself to visit the ladies' room, Quincy gave Serge the lowdown. Serge was delighted. From the moment Karen walked into his apartment earlier that night with Quincy, Serge had thought she was beautiful, and he had been struggling all night not to ogle her because she was Quincy's date. Serge begged Quincy to find an excuse and suddenly leave them. He assured Quincy that he would make sure Karen got home safely.

"The rest," Quincy said to Lena, "is history. They've been together ever since."

Lena thoroughly enjoyed double dating with Serge and Karen. She liked Karen right off. Karen was very friendly, and seemed to go out of her way to make Lena feel at ease.

Lena thought Karen was very pretty, and that she and Serge made a very handsome couple. Karen was tall, thin, and dark-complexioned like Serge. She wore her jet-black hair long and straight. Lena noticed the closeness between Karen and Serge immediately. They appeared to be best friends more than lovers.

The four of them had dinner at a great Italian restaurant in midtown, then walked over to Times Square and checked out a movie. When the movie was over, they strolled through the busy streets, laughing and joking with each other and making fun of some of the more ridiculous sights they saw in the city that never sleeps.

When Lena and Quincy dropped Karen and Serge off at Karen's apartment that night at midnight, Karen gave Lena her telephone number and suggested they get together without the guys to go shopping or to the movies. Lena was touched by her kindness, and promised to call her so they could get together.

Quincy knew that Lena was tired after the long day, so he drove her straight home. He walked her to her door.

"I like your friends, Quincy."

"Yeah? They like you, too."

"You think so?"

He took her hand. "I know so. They both told me that."

That made her happy.

"So what are you going to do tomorrow, angel?"

"I think I'll go to church tomorrow. I haven't gone in far too long, and I have a lot to be thankful for."

Quincy smiled at her. "You are positively the sweetest woman I have ever known." He shook his head in amazement. "You know, Lena, in the last two days I've been wrestling with myself about my feelings for you. You're so different from the women I've known, and I sometimes have to remind myself of that. I never . . . I've been a bachelor all my life, and I didn't have any plans to change that, but when I see you . . . Aw, Lena, when I'm with you, I can't think of anything else. I don't want to be with anyone else."

Quincy paused. He took a deep breath, then continued. "I'd like to make you a promise, Lena, that if you'll be my lady, if you allow me to be your man, I will never be unfaithful to you. If the way I feel now ever changed, I promise I'd tell you before I'd ever go behind your back. Will you be my lady?"

She could not breathe. *He promised he would never cheat on me.* "Yes, Quincy." Lena sighed, and tears of joy filled her eyes. She was not absolutely certain, but she thought she saw tears in Quincy's eyes before he covered her mouth with his.

FIFTEEN

Monday morning, when Quincy arrived at the bank, he ran into Cheryl in the lobby. He was in a jubilant mood because his weekend had been absolutely perfect. Although he did not see Lena on Sunday, they talked twice. First, when she called him after church, they were on the phone for almost two hours. Then he called to say good night. He went to sleep with a smile on his lips.

When Cheryl approached him that morning, her first words were, "I thought you were going to come to my party Friday night."

"Yeah, well, I couldn't make it," he answered.

"Why not? What were you doing?"

He looked at her strangely for a moment before he said, "I really don't think that's any of your business."

"Well, you missed a good one," she said indignantly.

"I don't think I missed anything. I had a fantastic weekend, and Friday night was the best part of it."

The elevator arrived and Quincy stepped into the car without another word to Cheryl. When he stepped off the elevator on his floor and spotted Lena at her desk, a broad smile crossed his face.

Cheryl was right on his heels. When he stopped at the reception desk to greet Lena, Cheryl also stopped. She said, "What's up, Lena?" but did not look at her for more than a split second. Then, without waiting for Lena to respond, she immediately turned to Quincy and said, "I need to meet with you today to go over the new benefits proposal."

Quincy took a deep breath and turned his head toward Cheryl. He looked at her with indifference and said, "Schedule it with Maritza." He immediately turned back to Lena and the smile instantly returned. "And how are you this morning, Lena?"

The tension in the air was thick. Lena's eyes darted from Quincy to Cheryl and back to Quincy. She smiled at him and answered, "I'm fine, Quincy. How are you?"

"Wonderful."

They both ignored Cheryl. They only had eyes for one another.

Cheryl sucked her teeth loudly, then turned in a huff and walked away.

Once there was no one in earshot, Quincy said, "You look beautiful this morning."

"Thank you."

During one of their conversations over the weekend, Lena and Quincy agreed that they would keep their relationship a secret on the job. Since Quincy was new to the bank, and in management, they felt it would be best if he did not appear to be involved with, technically, one of his subordinates. Despite that, however, there was no way he could walk past Lena if he was not working and not stop and talk to her. He just couldn't.

On Tuesday of the next week, Lena met Karen for lunch. Karen worked four blocks from the bank, so they met halfway and went to a Chinese restaurant.

They made small talk as they waited for their meals, but Karen noticed that almost every sentence Lena spoke was punctuated with Quincy's name.

"Lena, can I tell you something?"

"Sure, Karen. What?"

"Promise not to tell Quincy, cause I don't want Serge to know until I'm sure."

"I promise."

"I think I'm pregnant."

A broad smiled covered Lena's face. "That's wonderful. Congratulations."

"Thanks," Karen said with a smile, "but it's not definite yet."

"When will you know for sure?"

"I have an appointment with my doctor on Thursday," Karen said.

"Do you think you and Serge will get married?"

"I want to, but it seems like every time I mention the M word he gets all funny and quickly changes the subject."

"I'd like to marry Quincy." Lena then added, "But I doubt if that'll ever happen."

"Why do you say that?"

"I don't know. Quincy's so worldly. I don't think he'd want to marry someone like me. I've never even had sex," Lena said candidly.

"You haven't?"

"No. Quincy's my first real boyfriend. Before him, I was living in a bubble." Lena went on to tell Karen about her upbringing.

"I think Q's in love with you, Lena. I see the way he looks at you."

Lena hoped Karen was right.

"I'm in love with him."

Karen thought Lena's naiveté was sweet. "I know," Karen said with a smile. "It's written all over your face when you say his name."

Lena blushed.

"He's a good guy, Lena. I don't think you'll ever have to worry about him hurting you. He's a really good guy. He hooked me and Serge up."

Lena smiled brightly. "I know, he told me. What a great story."

"Serge is my soul mate. I can't even imagine my life with anyone else," Karen said honestly. "I would love to have his baby, too. But I want him to want it too, you know?"

"Yeah."

When Lena returned to the office, she called Quincy to see if he had returned from lunch yet. "Oh, you're back," she said when he picked up the phone.

"Yeah, I just went up to the cafeteria and picked up something. I saw Reggie upstairs, but he was with Cheryl and I didn't feel like listening to any of her bull, so I just brought it back and ate here. How was your lunch?"

"It was fun."

"How's Karen?"

"She's good. We went to that Chinese restaurant up the street, Royal Hunan. I like talking to her. She invited me to go with her this Saturday to a bridal shower."

"Oh yeah? Have you ever been to one?"

"No."

"I hear they can be really wild."

"Really?"

"Yeah. Don't let Karen corrupt you," Quincy said with a chuckle.

Lena laughed. "I won't."

"Listen, I have a game tonight at seven, but it's going to be at this school in the Bronx, so I'll be leaving at five tonight." Quincy usually got off at six. "Wait for me, okay?"

"Okay."

By Thursday of the following week Quincy had been dating Lena exclusively for three weeks, and he was happier than he had been in years.

That night, after having dinner with Lena and seeing her home, Quincy stopped by Serge's apartment. Serge had just purchased a fifty-inch television, and Quincy, who was considering a similar purchase, wanted to check it out.

"What's up, man?" Serge said when he opened the door. "You're just in time to catch the last quarter of the game."

"What's the score?" Quincy asked as he moved into the apartment with the familiarity of being at home.

"Seventy-five, seventy-three. Knicks."

Quincy dropped his jacket on the chair and moved to the kitchen to get something to drink. "You got any beer?"

"Yeah. Bring me one, too."

Quincy found the bottle opener and popped the tops off the two bottles, then headed back to the living room. As he handed a bottle to Serge, he said, "Damn, that's the bomb." He was referring to the television.

"Courtside seats," Serge responded. He took a long pull on his beer, then asked, "Where you coming from?"

"I just took Lena home. We had dinner at Puffy's place."

"How's she doing?"

"Great."

"Yo, Q, can I ask you a question without you getting mad?"

"What?" Quincy looked over at his friend skeptically. He had been poised to take a sip of his beer, but Serge's words halted his actions.

"Are you really serious about this girl, or are you just playing her?"

Quincy looked at Serge with impatience.

"I'm just asking 'cause she's not the type of woman you usually mess with, that's all," Serge explained.

"I'm serious." Quincy took a drink of his beer.

"Really?"

"What is it you want me to say, Serge?"

"No. It's just that, well, you haven't been serious about anyone since Rhonda, and Lena's . . . well, from what Karen tells me, Lena's very naive. You don't think the novelty of being with someone like her is going to wear off after a while? She seems like she'd be hurt real easy."

Quincy pondered what Serge had said for a moment before he responded. Lena was different from the women he usually associated with. Serge was right about that. And he could not explain why he felt for her the way he did. He just did.

"Lena's not a novelty, Serge. Yeah, she different, simply because she's the most sincere and unselfish person I know. She's on my mind twenty-four seven, man, and I can't explain why. I just know it feels good, and it feels right being with her."

"You're in love with her, aren't you?" Serge asked.

Quincy sighed. "Yeah."

"She seems like a nice lady. Karen likes her a lot."

"Yeah, she likes Karen, too."

"Maybe she's your soul mate," Serge suggested.

Quincy smiled. "Yeah, maybe."

"Have you been intimate with her?"

"No, and that's been a struggle, 'cause she turns me on so much. And I know if I asked her to, she would without a second thought."

"You think she's in love with you?"

"Yes, and I don't think she's ever been before."

"You've got to be careful with her."

"I know. I have been. The last thing I want to do is hurt her. You know, sometimes it scares me because my feelings for her are so strong. She's so totally open and eager to learn, and give, and live. She's like a baby in some respects, so I'm really careful about what I say and do when I'm with her." Quincy took a long sip of his beer. He rose from his seat and moved across the room to look out the window. "I've never felt this way before," he said softly. "It scares the hell out of me."

"Join the club. Karen's been hinting about marriage."

Quincy turned to face Serge. "So what are you going to do?"

"I don't know."

"Y'all have been together long enough. You're not going anywhere."

"I know. I just don't want things to change."

"What makes you think they will?"

"I don't know."

Quincy returned to the sofa and sat back down. He and Serge turned their attention back to the basketball game in progress, but neither of them was really watching it. They were contemplating their futures with the women in their lives.

SIXTEEN

On Friday of the following week, Quincy suggested to Lena that they go dancing after work. Since she couldn't dance, Lena had never been to a club and she was very reluctant to go now. With a bit of gentle persuasion, Quincy talked her into it, though. She was embarrassed that she did not know any of the latest dances, but he assured her that he didn't, either. He told her to just listen to the music and let it flow through her, that the rest would come naturally.

Lena was hesitant about getting out on the dance floor until it was so crowded that she was sure no one would be watching her. Once she got out there, though, there was no sitting her down. She had always been a big fan of rhythm and blues, and she liked the beats of some rap tunes, too. Being in that atmosphere with Quincy as her guide, and listening to the wonderful music booming from the massive speakers on the four corners of the dance floor, Lena discovered a brand-new joy.

By the time they were ready to leave the club, Lena was jubilant. She'd had the time of her life.

Quincy pulled into her block at 2:00 A.M. and

parked in front of her neighbor's house. As Lena was getting out of the car she said, "That was so much fun, Quincy. I hope I didn't embarrass you with my so-called dancing, though."

Quincy laughed. "You did just fine, Lena," he said, as he moved around the car to stand at her side.

Lena walked through her front gate after Quincy opened it. He followed her into the yard, but stopped before they reached the door.

Although they had been dating for a month and Quincy had been to her house on several occasions when picking her up for a date or driving her home, he had never spent any time there with her. "Lena, can I come in with you?"

She turned back to him and said with a smile, "Of course. I was hoping you would."

Quincy smiled.

The last month had flown by, and Quincy and Lena had grown very close. Although his strong physical attraction to her had not waned in the slightest, he was happy that their bond had grown stronger through time spent talking, laughing, and sharing. He found that he was able to be completely honest with Lena, and more candid than he usually was with anyone except Serge. Lena was an open vessel, eager to learn everything she could about life and those around her. And she was so giving. Her generosity often amazed him, and it only contributed to the growth of his love for her.

He had used kid gloves in dealing with her. Quincy seldom restrained himself when his physical attraction to a woman was so strong.

He was not sure how much longer he would be able to put up the front he had been. With each new day spent with Lena, the stronger his lust for her blazed. She just made him feel so good.

When they entered the house, Lena showed him into her living room.

"Have a seat, Quincy," she offered.

"Thanks."

"I'll be right back. I have to go to the bathroom."

Quincy sat on the sofa, but he caught sight of a picture of Lena when she was a little girl, and immediately rose to examine it. As he held the five-by-seven-inch frame he smiled, because she looked as if she had not aged a bit.

He placed the picture back on the table and studied one of a man and woman he assumed were Lena's parents. They were a very handsome couple, and Lena actually favored them both. She had her mother's dark skin and long hair, and she had her father's face.

"I'm sorry. I couldn't wait," Lena said as she reentered the living room.

He turned to her, "That's all right. Where is your bathroom?"

"Come here, I'll show you."

While Quincy was in the bathroom, Lena kicked off her shoes and turned on her stereo. She put a tape by Babyface in the deck.

"Quincy, would you like some lemonade?" she called, loudly enough for him to hear her through the bathroom door.

Quincy stepped out of the bathroom at that moment. "Sure, I'll have some. Thanks."

Lena went into the kitchen to pour them some of her freshly squeezed lemonade. She brought their drinks back into the living room. Quincy rose when she entered the room and took the two glasses from her and set them on the table.

"Come sit next to me," he said, as he reached for her hand. "You like Babyface, huh?"

"Yes."

"What woman doesn't?" he said with a smile. Then, "Yeah, he's cool, I guess. He definitely knows what to say."

Lena laughed and agreed. "I hear a lot of men feel that Babyface makes it hard for them by singing about all the things he wants to do for his woman."

"That's 'cause so many of them think it's weak to be in love that way."

"You don't feel that way?"

"No."

Lena picked up her drink then and took a sip. She noticed that Quincy had not touched his drink yet. Instead, he was staring at her with a playful smile.

"What?" she asked.

"What?" he responded.

"Why are you staring at me like that?"

"I'm sorry. I don't mean to make you uncomfortable. I just like looking at you."

"Drink your lemonade, Quincy."

"Yes, ma'am," he said as he picked up his glass and took a long sip. "Wow, this is good! Did you make this from fresh lemons?" he asked as he put the glass to his lips and finished it off.

"Yes, would you like some more?"

"Sure. I'd love some."

She took his glass and got up to refill it. As she walked away from him, he watched her small hips sway from side to side. He knew she was not doing it intentionally, but she was turning him on. When she returned with his drink, he was once again staring at her with the same little grin he'd worn before.

"What?"

"You know what? You are the sexiest woman I have ever known."

"Me!" she uttered in amazement.

"Yes, you."

"No one's ever told me that before," she said with a look of doubt.

"Well, I can't help it if everyone else is blind. Come here."

He reached out his hand and took the glass she was carrying and placed it on the table in front of them. Then he took her hand and pulled her down on his lap. He put his arms around her and kissed her softly on her neck.

"I am crazy about you, Lena Caldwell. Did you know that?" he whispered softly in her ear.

She looked into his eyes with love, but quickly cast hers down. She felt herself becoming misty-eyed.

He put his hand under her chin and raised her head. "Look at me. You're too pretty to be walking around with your head down. Hold your head up, angel. Let everybody see how beautiful you are."

She smiled shyly and said softly, "I've never known anyone like you."

"Well, the feeling's mutual."

He kissed her softly on her mouth, but the feel of her lips pressed against his was too much for him. He held her tighter and pushed his tongue between her lips and reveled in the sweet taste of her. Lena wrapped her arms around him and returned his kiss with equal fervor. Whenever he kissed her this way, Lena wondered if she felt as good to him as he did to her. After all, she was new at this romance stuff.

"I love you, Quincy," she heard herself say. She had been thinking it, but had not meant to say it out loud.

He took her face in his hands and smiled at her. "I love you, Lena."

He kissed her lips softly, then her cheeks, then her eyelids, then her lips again. He wanted to feel her body next to his. He wanted to feel her heart beating next to his. "Dance with me," he whispered.

The music was soft and mellow. Lena rose from his lap and stood before him. Quincy stood, too, and in the same breath he took her in his arms and held her tightly but tenderly. She wrapped her arms around his waist and laid her head on his chest. She had never been happier. *He loves me,* she thought. *He said he loves me.* Lena felt her eyes begin to tear, so she closed them in an effort to halt their flow. She squeezed him tighter, praying that she would never have to let him go.

Quincy kissed the top of her head and softly sang the words of the song to her. He loved the way she felt in his arms. His nerves were so sensitive at that moment that he could feel her hardened nipples pressed against his torso. When she looked up at him, he saw that her eyes were moist. He lowered his head to kiss her, and she stood on her toes to welcome it. Unconsciously, Quincy began to caress her body. He moved his hands slowly down her back as he pressed his erection against her warm welcoming form. Lena's hips swayed gently in time to the music and sent pleasure pulses through his body. Before long, they were grinding to the sensuous music that filled the air, lost in the heat of their emotions. Quincy's hands found their way to her backside with its perfect curves, and he massaged it skillfully, sending chills up her spine the likes of which she had never felt. Lena sighed in ecstasy. She felt a warm sensation in her loins, and knew from the many romance novels she had read that this was only a prelude to the pleasure she would encounter at Quincy's touch.

"You feel so good," he moaned. "I want you so much."

"Quincy, I love you." She sighed as she pressed her lips to his once again.

He hungered for her in a way he could not explain. His senses were jolted by the feel of her in his arms and the sweetness of her kiss. He wanted to devour her. Quincy rained kisses all over her face, her neck, and along her collarbone and shoulders.

His hands began to explore her body now in a different way. As Lena held him tightly, his hands found her breasts, and he caressed them, squeezing the soft mounds gently until she sighed in ecstasy. Quincy then slowly moved his hands downward along her sides until they were at her hips. He cupped her behind in his hands and pulled her closer so he could feel her pelvis pressed against his muscular thigh. One of his hands moved from her backside and found its way to her pubic area. He massaged her there gently, but with enough pressure so that it sent chills straight up her spine. Lena moved against him as he continued his ministrations, sighing from the feelings that coursed through her body, feelings she had never before experienced.

"Lena," Quincy sighed breathlessly, "I want to make love to you. I want to love you, angel."

Suddenly, Lena became anxious. Everything she felt was new to her, but it was all good. She had known, too, that they would reach this point eventually. She had known that if she continued to let him kiss her and touch her this way he would want more. In all honesty, she wanted more, too. Lena wanted to know what it felt like to be made love to, to feel a man inside her, as she had read about so many times in her books, but she was afraid. She figured it would be painful at first, but truthfully she was more afraid that she would not be able to make him feel the pleasure he made her feel.

"Quincy, wait," she said, and tried to pull away from him. "Wait."

heart&soul's got it all!

Motivation, Inspiration, Exhilaration!

FREE ISSUE RESERVATION CARD

YES! Please send my FREE issue of HEART & SOUL right away and enter my one-year subscription. My special price for 5 more issues (6 in all) is only $10.00. I'll save 44% off the newsstand rate. If I decide that HEART & SOUL is not for me, I'll write "cancel" on the invoice, return it, and owe nothing. The FREE issue will be mine to keep.

Name _____

      (First)   (Last)

Address _____ Apt.#

City _____ State _____ Zip _____ | MABP |

Please allow 6-8 weeks for receipt of first issue. In Canada: CDN $19.97 (includes GST). Payment in U.S. currency must accompany all Canadian orders. Basic subscription rate for 6 issues is $17.94.

BUSINESS REPLY MAIL

FIRST-CLASS MAIL   PERMIT NO. 272   RED OAK, IA

POSTAGE WILL BE PAID BY ADDRESSEE

heart&soul

P O BOX 7423
RED OAK IA 51591-2423

He did not release her right away. She had a feeling he had not even heard her. His kisses and caresses continued.

"No. Wait," she repeated. She pulled away from him completely and turned her back to him.

Quincy was so hot for her that he had not wanted to let her go. "What's the matter?" he asked with concern. *Am I going too fast?*

"I don't know," she said in a trembling voice. Tears he could not see were streaming down her face.

Quincy stepped closer to her and put his hands on her shoulders. "Talk to me, Lena. Tell me what's wrong."

Lena was ashamed of the way she felt. She felt like a child. She covered her face with her hands and cried softly. "I'm scared."

Quincy knew she had said something, but he could not make sense of her jumbled words. "What did you say? I didn't hear you."

"I said I'm scared," she cried.

"Why?" Quincy asked as he turned her to face him. "Do you think I would hurt you? I wouldn't hurt you, Lena."

She put her arms around him and held him close. She rested her head against his chest. "I never did it before," she whispered.

"What? You never did . . . ?" He stopped, and what she meant suddenly dawned on him. "You've never made love," he said, almost as a sigh.

"No," she cried, very upset.

Of course she's a virgin, you idiot. From everything he had learned about Lena, it made perfect sense. Quincy had never been with a virgin before, not even his first time. Suddenly he, too, was a little nervous. He did not want to hurt her.

"But why are you crying?"

"Because I feel so . . . so . . . like a baby!"

"Lena—"

"How many twenty-five-year-old virgins do you know?" she challenged.

"One," he answered softly. He took her face in his hands and tilted her head up to look at him. "You are one in a million, angel, and you have nothing to be ashamed of. Do you know how special that makes you?"

As she looked into his eyes tears continued to slide down her cheeks.

"Why would you want someone like me? I don't even know what to do."

"Lena, I love you. Don't you know that?"

"Yes."

"All I want is you. Do you know how proud it makes me feel to know that you have never been touched by any other man? I know it sounds a bit egotistical and chauvinistic, but that knowledge is very enticing. I want to make love to you, angel, but we don't have to do anything now if you don't want to. It won't change the way I feel about you. I'll still love you," he told her with great feeling, and he hugged her, because he did love her very much.

She held onto him tightly. "I want you to make love to me, but I don't know what to do to satisfy you. Will you show me?"

"Lena."

"Please? I don't want to disappoint you, Quincy."

"You could never do that. If you want me to show you what to do, I will. But I don't want you to be afraid of me. I want you to touch me. I don't want you to be afraid to touch me, all right?"

"All right."

He kissed her lips softly to show her how much he cared for her. His arms were wrapped around her waist. "You wanna know something funny? The day I met you . . . the day I interviewed for the job at the bank—"

"Uh huh."

"My horoscope for that day said I would meet someone who would cause a positive chain of events in my life. Of course, since I was going on that job interview I figured it was Dave Patterson, but I realized later that it was you. Only good things have happened to me since I've known you. You are beautiful, Lena, and I'm proud to be the man you want to share your innocence with. I don't want anyone else, sweetheart. I just want to be the best man I can be for you, and I want you to just be the beautiful you that you are."

As Lena looked up into his beautiful brown eyes, she knew she would always be safe with him. She stood on her toes, and put her arms up and around his neck. She pressed her lips to his.

In her wildest dreams Lena had never believed she could be as happy as she was when

she stood in Quincy's arms at that moment.
Months ago, she had been resigned to the fact
that she would never marry, or even have a boyfriend. But here she was in the arms of this wonderful, sensitive, too-good-to-be-true man who
confessed his love for her, who did not care that
she was not the kind of experienced woman he
was probably used to being with. She had been
positive that when he found out about her in-
experience he would change his mind about her
or make excuses about why they were not right
for each other, after all. But he had told her he
would never hurt her, and she believed him, believed that her heart was safe with him, that he
would be gentle with her the way he promised.
She wanted to make love with him. She wanted
him to be the man who showed her what it was
to be a total woman.

"Do you want to go upstairs?" he asked in a
soft voice when their lips parted.

"Yes."

Lena walked over to the stereo and turned it
off, then turned off the living room lights. She
reached for his hand in the darkness and
guided him to the stairs.

When they reached her bedroom she turned
to him and smiled nervously. He took her hand
and led her to the bed. He emptied his pants
pockets and placed his wallet on her dresser,
then sat down. She sat next to him.

"Don't be afraid, angel," he said softly as he
caressed her cheek.

"Okay," she panted.

"Do you want to take a shower?"

"Together?"

He smiled and said, "It's more fun that way."

Lena's heart was racing.

"Have you ever seen a man in the nude?" he suddenly asked her.

She looked over at him quickly, then turned her eyes away. "Not in person."

"Do you mind if I take your vest off?"

"No."

He began to lift the vest from her shoulders, and although she did not assist him she did not fight him, either. Once her vest was removed, he began to remove her top. He reached inside the waistband of her pants and pulled the tail of her blouse out, then slowly pulled it over her head and revealed her torso. She was wearing a white lace bra that snapped in front. He leaned across her to kiss her bare shoulder.

Lena watched as he placed soft kisses all across her shoulders and upper chest. His tender lips felt good against her skin, and without realizing what she was doing Lena found herself caressing the back of his head. He sat up after a time and gazed into her eyes. Without a word he slowly unsnapped her bra and bent over to kiss first one small bud, then the other. She sighed aloud as his tongue teased her again and again. He cupped her left breast in his hand and massaged it slowly until she moaned in delight. He planted a wet kiss on her mouth.

"How does that feel, Lena?" he murmured.

"Good," she said, out of breath.

"Would you help me out of my shirt?"

She reached over and began to unbutton his

shirt. He stared at her intensely the entire time. When she had reached his waistband, he stood up to afford her an easier time of undressing him. Lena pulled his shirt out of his pants without pause and continued to unbutton it. She pushed the shirt off his shoulders as soon as it was entirely unbuttoned. Quincy was not wearing an undershirt, so his chest was completely exposed. She was delighted to see that he was so muscular. His upper body appeared sculpted, and she found that very erotic.

"Touch me," he said softly.

Tentatively, Lena reached up and touched his pecs. She noticed that his nipples were hard, and that surprised her because she had not realized that men's bodies reacted similarly to women's when excited. She touched his nipples, curious to see how they felt. Quincy pulled her up from the bed gently. Lena stood before him, and he pulled the bra that he had unfastened minutes earlier off her shoulders and down her arms until it was completely off, and let it fall to the floor. Quincy wrapped his arms around Lena, and his heart leapt at the feel of her skin against his. She turned her head up to be kissed, and he happily obliged her. They stood there for almost five minutes, savoring their mutual love.

"Let's take off our pants," Quincy murmured.

"Okay," she said shyly.

Lena reached for the buckle of her belt. Quincy stopped her by taking her hands in his.

"You do me and I'll do you," he said.

She looked doubtfully into his eyes, but was

reassured by what she saw there. She reached for his belt and began to unbuckle it. He, in turn, began to unfasten her slacks. Quincy pushed them down and off her hips, then bent to take off her socks and pull each leg out of the pants.

As she stood before him in her panties, Quincy took Lena's hands and placed them on his waist. He then guided her hands and helped her remove his pants.

Seconds later, Quincy stood in front of Lena clad only in his briefs. As his erection strained for freedom from its cotton confines, Lena tried to keep her eyes riveted to his chest, but she was so curious about the bulge in his underwear that they kept wandering there. Quincy saw her struggling not to look at him. He took one of her hands in his and held it at their sides for a moment. He slowly brought it up then, and before she realized what he was doing he had placed her hand directly on his crotch. Lena's first instinct was to pull away, and she tried to, but he held her hand in place.

"Lena, don't be afraid to touch me," he said softly. She was still trying to pull away from him when he repeated, "Don't be afraid to touch me."

After a few seconds, Lena relaxed and began to concentrate on how he looked and felt against the palm of her hand. His penis felt massive against her tiny hand, and—although she was a bit more apprehensive about this whole thing now—she was also very excited about being able to touch him this way. And, despite the fact that she had nothing to compare it to, she thought it looked big, too.

"I won't hurt you, Lena," he whispered.

Suddenly, Quincy slid his briefs off and stood before her in the nude. Lena took a deep breath and expelled it loudly. Her senses were very acute at that moment. She was even more excited by the sight of his naked body. He was absolutely beautiful. He looked like the perfect male specimen. His penis looked even bigger than it had when he had on his underwear. She had never seen a real one before, and found that she could not take her eyes off it. She was fascinated by the shape of it—long and thick, with fat veins running just beneath the smooth brown skin. It made her think of a gun, the way the shaft was connected to the small sac at its base, and appeared to challenge her as it stood straight out from the thick curly hair that surrounded it. The bulbous head reminded her of a hat of sorts.

He stepped closer to her and began to slide her panties off her hips. She stood where she was and let him do as he pleased, watching his eyes as he removed her panties. He had such an intense look in his eyes, almost as if he had waited for her forever. He pulled her close so that their bodies touched. Lena was immediately excited by the feel of his flesh against hers. She held him tightly and pressed herself against the erection that she had been fearful of just moments ago. She'd never known such physical closeness could feel so good. Lena could not believe what she had been missing all these years.

"You feel so good to me, Quincy," she moaned.

"Mmm, you feel good, too. But this is only the beginning. I'm going to make you feel things you've never felt before, and I'll make sure you love every minute of it."

"I know you will, Quincy. I love you."

"I love you, my precious Lena."

He kissed her lips softly for a couple of seconds before he said, "Let's go take a shower."

She led him to the bathroom that was connected to her bedroom.

Quincy stepped over to the shower stall, turned on the faucet, and adjusted the water temperature until it was comfortable for them. "After you, my lady love."

Lena stepped into the stall and moved aside to allow him to enter. He stepped in behind her and closed the stall door. At once, he embraced her and tilted his head to kiss her. Lena stood on her toes to welcome his kiss eagerly.

She felt like a dream in his arms. Quincy could think of nothing he had ever felt that compared to the feel of her wrapped in his arms, her naked body pressed against his.

His hands traveled down her back and found her soft round backside. He squeezed her cheeks and pulled her closer to him. His leg was pressed between hers, and she rubbed her center against the muscles of his thigh.

A familiar pulsing began between Lena's legs. This feeling was soon followed by one she had never felt before. It washed over her, and she cried out uncontrollably. Lena pressed herself harder against him and moaned in delight, sounding more surprised than satisfied. "I think . . . I'm . . . having—"

"Yes, Lena." Quincy sighed. "You feel good. You feel so good, angel."

Teeth clenched, she could speak no longer. The feeling seemed to be building in intensity. She squeezed him harder, and his hold on her tightened, as well.

Quincy wanted nothing more, at that moment, than to penetrate her, to feel her warmth surround him, but he knew he could not do that with her. He had to go slowly, though he was incredibly turned on by her. He tried to think of something else to take his mind off of what she was making him feel.

Quincy reached behind her and grabbed one of her legs in his hand. He raised her foot off the floor of the shower. Lena held fast to his strong body, so he took his other hand and placed it between her legs. She jumped a bit at his first touch there, but relaxed quickly as he parted her lips to explore her warmth. Lena's heart raced faster with each gentle stroke.

Quincy fondled her for almost ten minutes and introduced her to a whole new world of physical love before they separated to wash each other's bodies. Lena no longer felt fearful of Quincy's penis. Instead, she was fascinated by it. She held it gently and stroked it, almost absentmindedly, studying its shape, size, and texture. He did not think she even realized what she was doing to him. He closed his eyes, threw his head back, and shook it from side to side as opposed to screaming out his pleasure.

"Lena, Lena, Lena."

"Am I doing it right?" she asked innocently.

"Oh, yes. Oh, yes, Lena. Aw, you're doing it so right," he panted.

"It's so smooth. I like the way it feels," she told him.

"Ooh, I like the way it feels, too."

She realized then how much she was satisfying him, and she was happy.

"I love you, Quincy," she breathed with her mouth at his ear.

"Oh, Lena, I can't wait to feel you." His voice had changed, having taken on a deeper, rougher tone.

When they stepped out of the shower twenty minutes later, they took their time drying each other's bodies.

"Do you have any body lotion?" he asked.

"Yes."

"Well, I'll rub you down, and then you can do me, okay?"

She smiled and said, "Okay."

Quincy led her to her bed, and she lay on her stomach. He poured the lotion into his hand, then rubbed his hands together before he began to massage it into her skin. He took his time, starting at her feet and slowly working his way up to her neck.

Lena was so aroused by the way he touched her that she climaxed for the second time in her life.

Quincy was trying hard not to lose control. Lena had him in such a state that before he realized what he was doing he was kissing her between her legs. He had never performed oral sex, but with Lena he could not help himself. She screamed with joy when she felt his tongue invade her private garden of love.

Once he had drunk his fill of her, he turned her over and began to massage her front. As he rubbed the lotion over her body, he lingered at her breasts longer than anywhere else on her body, taking them in his mouth and sucking on them like a newborn babe.

When he had completed his body rub, he leaned over her and whispered in her ear, "Okay, now it's my turn."

She lay there with a smile on her face and said, "Lie down."

Quincy moved off her and lay on the bed, facedown.

Lena took the lotion from her dresser and put a dab in her hand. She gently took one of his feet in her hands and began to rub the lotion on it. She thought he had nice feet for a man, and she kissed each foot after applying the lotion. She spread the lotion slowly up one leg and then the other, sending chills through his body at her touch. He knew she had never done this before, but she took her time, and so far she was batting a thousand.

He moaned at the feel of her hands on his backside, kneading his cheeks as if they were dough. He almost fell asleep from the gentle way she massaged his back.

"Turn over," she whispered in his ear.

He quickly obliged. He lay there with his legs spread slightly apart. His distended member rested on his lower abdomen, the tip coming up to meet his navel. Lena applied lotion to every part of him except his manhood.

"I think you forgot a spot," he joked.

She laughed softly and said, "No, I didn't. I was saving the best for last."

"I'm glad."

She poured some lotion into her hand then took his erection in hand. She massaged his penis and testicles slowly, gently, with intense concentration. Quincy writhed on the bed. He was so aroused by her and wanted her so much that the feel of her hands on him, touching him the way she was, made him feel as though he would climax at any moment.

"Stop. Lena, stop," he said, breathing heavily.

"Did I do something wrong?"

"Oh, God no, angel. You didn't do anything wrong. You're doing everything right. I just felt like I was going to come. I don't want to do that yet."

"I'm sorry."

"Oh, no, please don't be. You're beautiful, Lena, and I love the way you touch me. Your hands are so warm, and they feel so good. Don't apologize. You're wonderful," he said with a smile as he reached out to caress her face.

Lena stretched out on top of him and kissed him softly. He put his arms around her and stuck his tongue in her mouth, delighting in the sweetness of her. She moved on him, and continued to send him to unparalleled heights.

His hands moved across her backside gently as he caressed her, then moved steadily across her skin until they had parted her legs. As Lena rubbed against his swollen member, Quincy arched his hips and moved them sensuously, then he placed two fingers into her love canal. She climaxed yet again, screaming out his name as the feel of him pressed against her love button, combined with his gentle touch, drove her to the brink.

"I want to feel you, Lena. I want to feel you on me," he moaned. "Are you ready for me?"

"Yes. Yes, Quincy. I want you to make love to me," she said in a tiny voice, sighing.

He turned her gently so that she was now on her back. He reached over to the dresser, grabbed his wallet, and quickly opened it to remove a condom.

"Would you put this on for me?"

He knelt over her. Lena took the condom from him, and under his direction she placed it on his penis. She opened her legs, now wanting to feel him as much as he wanted her. She was no longer afraid that he would hurt her. She knew she was safe in his arms, that as long as she had him, no one could hurt her.

Quincy gently lay on top of her and rested his weight on his hands. He lowered his head and kissed her hungrily, nibbling her neck and ears and causing her to move her hips underneath him in anticipation of what was to come.

In the next seconds, Quincy took his manhood in hand and guided it to her opening.

"Tell me if I'm hurting you, Lena, and I'll stop," he said breathlessly.

The feel of her moist lips against the head of his penis was so delicious that he grunted uncontrollably. He pushed slowly, and felt her cushiony softness giving way for him to enter her.

Lena seemed to hold her breath at the initial feel of his manhood at the door of her secret garden. She tensed involuntarily.

"Relax, baby. Relax," he urged.

He continued to push, and was intoxicated by the reality of becoming a part of her. She was tight, but that was to be expected. She was warm, and she was wet, and she was driving him insane. He was pleasantly surprised when she arched her hips up to allow him more leverage, and before he knew it he was completely inside of her.

"Oh, Quincy! Oh! Oh!" she yelled breathlessly.

"Lena," he growled. He felt as if he would explode in her at any second. He could not believe how good she felt. She was moving against him slowly, and he loved every second of it.

"Wait! Wait, baby. Don't move. Please, don't move," he moaned in her ear. He did not want to come, not yet, but he had never felt anything that good in his life.

The sensation caused by him filling her up the way he did was indescribable. When Lena felt him push that last time, she had come up to meet him halfway, although it was uncomfortable at first. She knew the moment he was completely inside of her. She felt the pressure against the walls of her canal, but the friction caused by her tightness was incredibly intoxicating. She held him tightly, knowing she did not want that good feeling to ever stop. She moved against him slowly, loving the feel of his hard body mingling with hers. When he asked her to stop moving, she couldn't. She was having yet another orgasm.

"Quincy! Quincy! Oh my God! Oh my God!" she cried.

He held her tightly, knowing that she was climaxing again. He began to stroke her with a new fervor, and she met him thrust for thrust. They made love with reckless abandon. Quincy forgot for a moment that she was inexperienced. He loved the way she let her inhibitions go, giving herself up to the feelings that coursed through her. But he did not know that she was happier than she had ever been in her life.

Lena prayed that she would not lose him. She was not sure what she would do if she ever lost Quincy. She began to cry. She was so overcome with emotion that she could not help herself.

Unbeknownst to her, Quincy was experiencing something that he had never felt. He had been in love before, but never like this. He was so moved by the way she felt to him and the way she made him feel that his eyes began to water.

"I love you, Lena," he whispered in her ear.

"I love you, Quincy. I'll always love you."

SEVENTEEN

It was just past nine-thirty when Quincy opened his eyes Saturday morning. He smiled at the sight of Lena sleeping comfortably beside him. Immediately his thoughts returned to their night of love. It had been the greatest night of his life. They'd had intercourse for only a short time, but those had been the best minutes of his life. He'd only had the one condom, and was annoyed with himself because he had wanted to make love to her over and over, all night long. After he was spent, though, they had passed the next hour or so kissing, touching and exploring each other's bodies. Lena was eager to please, and he delighted in that, but he also loved the way she responded to his touch. He was amazed at how good she felt, and he was glad he had not hurt her, at least he didn't think he had. She had followed his lead, and after a while had just let herself go. Lena had opened herself up to him and allowed him to love her the way he wanted because she knew he was capable of fulfilling her every desire. She was a quick study, too, he was delighted to find. She'd touched him in all the right places, as if she had already known what to do and, although he had not been able to penetrate her a second time, she had expertly brought him to his peak once again.

She stirred then, flexing her body like a cat, poking her behind up under the covers until she was all stretched out. When she relaxed, she opened her eyes and looked right into his.

"Good morning," he said softly, with a smile.

She grinned and said, "Good morning."

They stared into each other's eyes for a few seconds without a word.

Finally, Quincy asked, "How are you feeling?"

"Like I just lost my virginity."

They both laughed.

"Did you enjoy last night?" he asked.

She reached over, grabbed him, and pulled her body closer to his. "Last night was wonderful. Thank you for making my first time so special."

"The first time should always be special, but every subsequent occasion should be, too, and I promise you they will." He kissed her lips softly and continued, "My only regret is that I don't have any more protection. I really want to make love to you right now. Can't you tell?"

She could feel his swollen member pressed against her leg.

"I was wondering for a moment if you had brought a club to bed with us," she joked.

"Yes. The same one I always carry."

They laughed and joked for a few minutes more until Quincy wrapped her in a warm embrace and said, "I love you, Lena. Where have you been all my life?"

She smiled and answered, "Seems like I've been hiding from you, and everything else in the world."

"Well, we're gonna change that."

"Will you be my personal tour guide?" she asked demurely.

"My pleasure, ma'am."

When they finally got out of bed they showered together, and then Lena went downstairs to prepare their breakfast. She was cooking pancakes and bacon. When Quincy entered the kitchen, Lena was stepping out to dump the garbage.

"Give me that, baby. I'll take it out," he said, and took the bag from her. "Where do you put it, out in front?"

"Yeah. The can's right inside the gate."

"Okay."

Quincy walked out the back door and along the side of the house to the front yard. He was wearing his slacks and shirt from the day before, but the shirt was unbuttoned and hung carelessly out of his pants. When he reached the front of the house he noticed that Lena's next-door neighbor was in her yard. She was an older woman, about his mother's age, and she stared at him curiously. He tried to ignore her but couldn't, so he smiled and said, "Good morning."

The woman was caught off guard, and the surprise registered on her face before she recovered and responded, "Good morning."

Quincy could not help but smile to himself as he walked around the back and reentered the house. As he stepped into the kitchen, he was chuckling softly about it.

"What's so funny?" Lena wanted to know.

"I just met one of your neighbors."

"Where?"

"The house next door," he said, pointing to the right.

"Oh, that's Mrs. Washington. She used to be a friend of my mother's."

"Yeah? Well, she looked real surprised to see me."

"I'm sure she was. No men ever come here to visit me. And you went out there like that. Shoot, she's probably thinking, 'That Lena done gone wild since her mother died.' She's real nosy. She'll probably be out there when we go out."

"You think so?"

"I'd bet money on it. She'll probably ask me if you're my boyfriend, too."

"No, she won't," Quincy said with a chuckle.

"Yes, she will. I'm telling you, she's real nosy."

It was almost two o'clock when Lena and Quincy walked out her door on their way to Brooklyn. Quincy wanted to change his clothes, and they were planning to take in a movie later that night. Lena had packed an overnight bag, since she was going to spend the night at his apartment.

To his surprise, Mrs. Washington was sitting in her front yard when they came out, just as

Lena had predicted. He turned to Lena with a smile and she whispered, "I told you."

The weather was very warm, and her neighbor sat in a lawn chair with a big straw hat on her head and dark glasses on her eyes, pretending to read the book she held in her hands.

As they reached the gate and were about to walk through, she called out, "Hello, Lena."

"Hi, Mrs. Washington," Lena replied as she turned to her neighbor. "How are you?"

"I'm fine, honey. How you been doin'?"

"Fine, thank you."

Lena and Quincy continued to his car, which was parked right in front of Mrs. Washington's house. Quincy had stepped over to the passenger side to open the door for Lena when Mrs. Washington called out, "Is that your boyfriend, Lena?"

Lena looked at Quincy with a grin and murmured, "told you" to Quincy before she turned and answered. "Yes. This is Quincy Taylor. Quincy, this is Mrs. Washington."

"Hello, Mrs. Washington. Nice to meet you," Quincy said cordially.

"Hello, son. It's nice to meet you, too," the woman said as she looked over her glasses at him.

Quincy then walked around to the driver's side and climbed in. Once they were both seated and had closed the doors, they burst into laughter.

"Damn, Lena, I can't believe she asked you that," Quincy said.

"I told you. She's real nosy, and doesn't hesitate to ask anyone anything. She probably saw your car parked out here and was wondering whom it belonged to. She knows everybody on the block, and whose car belongs to whom. I know she was shocked to see you this morning, and probably even more shocked to find out that this is your car—especially since it's been here all morning."

"Damn, y'all got your own neighborhood watch with her, huh?"

"That's for sure."

He started the car, and as they pulled off he asked, "Do you drive?"

"Uh-huh."

"Oh, that's good."

"My father's old car is in the garage," she told him.

"Do you ever drive it?"

"Yeah, but only to the supermarket and back. Before I met you, I didn't have anyplace else to go." She looked over at him with a smile.

"What kind of car is it?"

"A nineteen eighty-three Cadillac Coupe de Ville."

"Yeah? And it runs okay?"

"Uh-huh. The engine kicks in without any problems."

"Well, now you have someplace besides the supermarket to drive it. You can come and visit me in Brooklyn."

"I sure can."

"You can handle a big car like that with no problems?"

"Yup."

He glanced at her with a wicked smile and said, "That doesn't surprise me. You handled me with no problems."

She looked over at him and smiled.

EIGHTEEN

Quincy lived on the seventh floor of a ten-story condominium in downtown Brooklyn. His apartment had a large living room, a modern kitchen and dining area, two bedrooms—one of which he used as an exercise room and den—and a large bathroom with a tub and separate shower stall.

The living room was stylishly furnished. His seating arrangement was in black leather with smoked glass and brass accent tables. In the middle of the highly polished parquet floor was a black-and-tan zebra-striped area rug. On one wall was a black lacquer wall unit that held a sophisticated stereo system, a twenty-five-inch color television, and a few family portraits and knickknacks. A small étagère of smoked glass and brass held numerous basketball trophies.

"Come on in, sweetie. Make yourself at home," Quincy told her as they entered the apartment.

"This is nice, Quincy," Lena said as she looked over the room. "Did you decorate it yourself?"

"Yeah. You like it?"

"Yes, I do. You have nice taste."

"Thanks. Let me take your jacket and bag."

She handed him her overnight bag, and as she removed her jacket he told her, "You can look around, if you like. You might as well get to know where everything is. You're not a guest here."

She smiled at him and said, "Not even on my first visit?"

"Nope. Do you want anything to drink?"

"No, thank you. Not right now."

She took a seat on his sofa. As he hung her jacket in the closet she said, "Nice bear you have here." She picked up the stuffed bear she had won for him at the amusement park last month. Quincy had it propped on his sofa.

"Yeah? This really beautiful lady I'm seeing gave me that."

"She must think you're pretty special."

"Well, I don't know. But I'll tell you, she's the best thing that's ever happened to me." He winked at her as he closed the closet door, then said, "Turn on the television or the stereo, if you like."

"Okay."

She set the bear back on the sofa, got up, and walked over to his wall unit. She was fascinated by the large number of compact discs he had, and as she began looking through them she noticed that they were all stored in alphabetical order.

"Have you ever counted how many discs you have?" she asked him.

"I stopped after one fifty," he told her honestly.

"Oh my goodness."

"I'm gonna go change. I'll be right back," he said.

"Okay."

"If you want anything in the fridge, help yourself."

"Thank you."

She noticed that he had a large assortment of oldies, so she put on a disc that featured some of the greatest R&B hits from 1979.

As she was about to sit back on the sofa, she heard a rhythmic banging on his front door. It sounded as if someone were using his door as a drum.

"Quincy, I think someone's at your door," she called.

He came out of his bedroom with only his pants on. "It's probably Serge. No one else beats on my door like that." He walked to the door and, without asking who was there or looking through the peephole, opened it.

"What's up, man? Where you been? We were supposed to be playing Mike and them today, remember?" Serge said as he walked into the apartment.

"Oh, man, I forgot. I completely forgot," Quincy said, putting one hand to his head.

"Yeah, well, you owe me twenty dollars. I had to pay them fools since you didn't show up," Serge told him with his hand out.

"Hey, man, I'm sorry. I really forgot about it. But you owed me twenty dollars, anyway, so now we're square," Quincy said with a smirk.

"Yeah, all right, if that's the way you wanna be."

Quincy laughed.

"Hey, Lena. What's up?" Serge said.

Lena smiled. "Not much, Serge. How are you?"

"I'm okay." He then turned to Quincy and said, "Well, at least I can understand why you forgot."

"Hey. Some things are just more important than others, you know," Quincy said as he headed back to his bedroom to finish changing his clothes.

"I can dig it," Serge responded. "So how you been, Miss Lena?"

"Pretty good. I can't complain."

"Doesn't help, anyway."

"That's true. How's Karen?"

"She's good." Serge dropped down on the sofa heavily. "Man, I'm whipped. I just got through playing ball. I was out there since ten o'clock this morning. If I had known you were gonna be here, I would have showered before I came over."

She smiled and said, "That's okay."

"Quincy told me you guys were going to the movies last night. What'd you see?"

"Oh, we didn't go to the movies. We went dancing. It was fun. I'd never been to a night club before."

"You're kidding, right?"

"No. I've led a very sheltered life up to now."

Serge knew that. Quincy had told him quite a bit about Lena's background. At first he thought Quincy was out of his mind for even becoming involved with someone as naive as Lena was, but as he got to know her personally he came to understand Quincy's attraction to her. Serge thought she was a very sweet lady, and just what his best friend needed.

"We thought about calling you and Karen, but it was so last-minute. Besides, I know I embarrassed Quincy with my nondancing self. I wouldn't want to embarrass you, too."

"Oh well, you wouldn't have to worry about that. Quincy's been clubbing for years, and he can't dance, either."

Lena laughed.

Serge said, "Excuse me a minute."

He walked out of the living room, then, and to the bathroom.

Lena liked Serge. She thought he was cute. He looked a lot younger than Quincy, though. She thought he looked closer to her age, actually.

"Where's Serge?" Quincy asked when he returned to the living room.

"In the bathroom."

"Are you hungry?" he asked Lena.

"A little."

"I was thinking about ordering some Chinese food or a pizza. Which would you rather have?"

"Pizza."

Just then Serge reentered the living room. "Hey y'all, guess what?"

"What?" they chorused.

"Karen's pregnant."

"Yeah? Congratulations!" Quincy said with a genuine smile.

"Congratulations!" Lena echoed. *So, it's official now,* she thought. She remembered when Karen had told her of her suspicion two weeks ago.

"Yeah, thanks," Serge mumbled.

"What's the matter? Aren't you happy?" Quincy asked.

"Yeah, I guess so."

Quincy looked at Serge skeptically, then at Lena sardonically.

"They've only been going out together for about four years," he said to Lena.

"I know. Karen told me."

"What is it? Are you scared?" Quincy asked Serge.

"Yeah, man. Wouldn't you be?"

"Yeah, I guess. How does Karen feel?"

"She's ecstatic."

"I'm sure. When's she due?"

"November." Serge sighed, then said, "I'm kinda happy. Hey, I'm thirty-three years old. It's about time, don't you think?"

"Yeah, I do."

"Yeah, well, what are you waiting for?"

"Lena and I have only known each other— what—two and a half months?" Quincy asked, looking at Lena.

She answered, "Three, if you count when we first met."

He smiled at her. "Ain't she cute?" Quincy said to Serge.

Serge just snickered.

"Yo, man, you know you ain't goin' nowhere. And to be perfectly honest with you, you'd be a fool if you even thought about it. Karen is a great person. You've got a good woman. If you were smart, you'd do the right thing and marry her," Quincy told his friend.

"Yeah, I know. I've been thinkin' about that."

"Hey, listen, are y'all doing anything later on? Lena and I are goin' to the movies. Why don't y'all come with us?"

"What are you gonna see?"

"I don't know. What d'you wanna see, sweetie?" Quincy asked Lena.

"I don't care. You know I don't care," she answered.

"Why don't y'all come with us?" Quincy asked Serge again.

"All right. I'll call Karen and see if she feels like it."

"Hey, I'm gonna order a pizza. You hangin' out for a while?"

"Nah, I'ma go home and change. What time are you going out?"

"Probably not until about six or seven."

"All right, I'll come back here. If anything comes up, I'll call you."

"Bet."

"You're goin' into the city, right?" Serge asked.

"Yeah."

"Oh, all right. I'll see you later then. See ya' later, Lena."

"Okay, Serge. Bye."

As Quincy locked the door behind Serge,

Lena asked him, "How long have you guys known each other?"

"Oh, I don't know. Seems like forever."

"That's nice. I wish I had a best friend like that."

"I'll be your best friend," he said, as he walked over to her and pulled her up from the couch.

"You will?" she asked as she wrapped her arms around his waist.

"Oh, most certainly," he said, and bent to kiss her lips. When their lips parted, Quincy sighed. "That was nice."

"Mmm, yes it was," she whispered.

"You know we've got a few hours before we go out. Do you still want me to order that pizza, or would you rather we pass the time in a different way?"

"What do you have in mind?" she asked, knowing all too well what he wanted.

"I'd really like to spend the afternoon making love with you, if that's all right."

"Do you have more condoms?"

"Oh yeah. I have got a supply of them here," he said with a chuckle.

"Really? Do you use them that frequently?" Lena asked.

"No, ma'am. As a matter of fact, I haven't used them in a couple of months."

"Well, in that case, Quincy, I'd really like to make love to you, too."

He gazed into her eyes and smiled.

"I love you," he said softly.

"I love you."

"Come on, I'll show you my bedroom," Quincy said as he led her to the back of the apartment.

NINETEEN

Lena spent Saturday night with Quincy at his place, but because she had only brought a change of clothes for one day, they ended up back in the Bronx at her house on Sunday. They left from there to go to work on Monday morning.

When they arrived at their building, they walked through the lobby holding hands. They were standing in the corner of the elevator bank whispering and laughing when Cheryl Stewart stepped up to the elevator bank. She spied Quincy and Lena in the corner and made her way through the waiting crowd to confront them.

"Well, good morning," she said with a hint of sarcasm.

They had not even seen her approach because they were so wrapped up in each other.

"Good morning," they said in unison.

"I thought you were coming out with us Friday to celebrate Reggie's birthday," Cheryl said to Quincy.

"Had other plans," Quincy said flippantly.

"What other plans?" Cheryl demanded.

Quincy looked at her as if she were crazy. "That's none of your business."

The bell on the elevator nearest them rang, and the doors opened.

"Come on, Lena," Quincy said as he placed an arm around her waist and walked with her into the elevator. As Cheryl followed them, she noticed the way Quincy held Lena. Cheryl was very resentful of the attention he paid her. As the elevator filled, Quincy moved to the back of the car, and Lena stood directly in front of him. Cheryl moved to the opposite corner of the car and pretended to ignore them. She noticed, however, when he bent his head to whisper in Lena's ear, and the broad smile that crossed her face at his words.

Cheryl surmised that he had slept with her. *That bitch told me she wasn't interested in him,* she thought. Cheryl decided that she would confront Lena when she ran into her in the ladies' room. She was sure she could convince Lena that she was no match for Quincy.

When they reached their floor, they exited the elevator and walked through the corridor toward the reception area. Lena stepped behind her desk and Quincy stopped for a moment. Cheryl walked past them, but glared at Lena.

"I think she's mad at me," Lena said.

"Yeah? Well, she'll get over it," Quincy responded.

"I didn't tell you this before, but she told me that she was interested in you.

"That's too bad."

"She asked me if I was interested in you."

"What did you tell her?"

"I told her no at the time, even though it was a lie."

He grinned at her, but did not comment.

"She said she didn't want to put any moves on you if I was interested, but since I wasn't she was planning to. She also asked me if I was a virgin."

"What!" Quincy was shocked and disgusted by Cheryl's gall.

"Yeah."

Quincy sucked his teeth and said, "If she asks you anything else about you or me or us, tell her to mind her damn business!"

"I couldn't tell her that, Quincy."

"Then let me know. I'll tell her," he said with a scowl.

"I don't want to start anything," Lena beseeched.

"She's the one that's starting it. Lena, don't let her walk all over you."

"I won't."

Just then, Maritza stepped off the elevator and walked through the reception area.

"Good morning," she said cheerfully.

"Good morning, Maritza," Lena answered with a smile.

"Hey, Maritza. How are you?" Quincy asked.

"I'm fine. How was your weekend?"

They answered in unison, "It was wonderful!"

Quincy and Lena burst into laughter.

Maritza smiled knowingly. "That's nice. I'm glad you both had such a nice . . . weekend."

"How was yours?" Quincy smirked.

"Not as good as yours," she said, and continued on her way.

"Hey, let me get back there," Quincy said to Lena. "I'll see you at lunchtime."

"Okay," Lena said with a grin.

Cheryl did not have an opportunity to speak to Lena until it was almost time to go home. Every time she ran into her during the day, she was with Quincy or someone else was around.

She told Bernadette about seeing Quincy and Lena that morning and expressed her displeasure about the whole situation. Bernadette thought she was making a big deal out of nothing. She told Cheryl she should just forget about Quincy. "After all," she said, "there are plenty of other men in this city, and he ain't all that."

Cheryl was upset because of the way Quincy shot her down when she asked what he had been doing on Friday, and because he seemed to fawn over Lena. He barely even looked at her anymore. She was determined that if she could not have Quincy, she would make sure that poor, little, timid Lena regretted going behind her back the way she had.

Cheryl was standing in the corridor speaking with a coworker when she spotted Lena going into the ladies' room. "Excuse me a minute, Walter. Nature calls," Cheryl said, and immediately turned away from him and toward the ladies' room.

She was carrying her purse, so when she saw that Lena was still in one of the stalls she pulled out her makeup bag, stood at the sink in front of the mirror, and began to touch up her face.

After a minute or two Lena emerged from the stall, and Cheryl could see from her reflection that she was surprised to see her standing there.

"Hi, Cheryl."

Cheryl turned to her and looked her up and down. "What's up?" she said dryly.

Lena tried to ignore the ominous look Cheryl was giving her as she washed her hands, but her stomach knotted in anticipation of what she would say. She was positive it would have something to do with Quincy.

Sure enough, not even ten seconds had passed when Cheryl started. "I thought you told me you weren't interested in Quincy."

Lena looked over at Cheryl, not knowing how to respond.

Suddenly, she became anxious and her heart began to race. She could tell that Cheryl was angry. She wore a scowl on her heavily made up face, and had positioned herself near the door with her hand on her hip, making it almost impossible for Lena to pass.

When Lena did not respond, Cheryl raised her voice. "Didn't you hear me talking to you?"

"What do you want me to say?" Lena asked nervously.

At that moment, two of their coworkers walked in. Lena let go a sigh of relief.

"Hey, ladies," one of the women said.

"Hi, Mary," Lena said with a bright smile. "How are you?"

"I'm fine, Lena. How're you?"

"I'm good. Hi," she said to the other woman as a courtesy. She didn't really know her.

Cheryl didn't acknowledge either woman.

Lena immediately saw her opportunity to get away from Cheryl. "Excuse me," she said, as she brushed by Cheryl and Mary on her way to the door.

"I'll talk to you later, Lena," Cheryl said sweetly.

Lena looked back at Cheryl, and could see the anger in her eyes as she pulled open the door. She did not respond.

When Lena stepped out of the ladies' room, she noticed Quincy walking toward her in the corridor.

"Hey, you," he said.

"Hi." Her heart was still racing from her confrontation with Cheryl.

"You wanna go get something to eat before we go home?"

"I thought you had a game tonight," she said. Quincy played on the bank's basketball team now.

"It's been canceled."

Just then, Quincy saw Cheryl emerge from the ladies' room behind Lena. When Cheryl noticed him, she quickly averted her eyes and turned in the opposite direction.

"Did she say something to you?" he asked sternly.

"Who?" She knew he was speaking of Cheryl, despite the fact that she'd never turned.

"Cheryl."

"No," Lena answered, and immediately began to move past him.

He grabbed her arm gently to halt her movement. "Tell me the truth, Lena."

"She didn't say anything," Lena lied. She didn't want to tell Quincy what had just happened because she knew he would definitely confront Cheryl about it, and she didn't want him to know that she was such a wimp.

The next day, Lena called and asked Karen to meet her for lunch. She tried her best all morning to avoid contact with Cheryl. The reception desk was actually the best place she could be, since it was right out in the open. She was happy, too, that Quincy was ignorant of what was going on. She knew he'd have a fit.

When Lena and Karen met in the park across the street, she told Karen about Cheryl for the first time.

When Lena was finished with her narrative, Karen simply said, "You'd better check that witch."

"Karen, she made me feel as if she wanted to fight me. I don't want to fight her."

"That's why you have to check her. You have to let her know that Quincy is your man, and she needs to get over it and get a life. Who does she think she is, anyway? What? Does she think that because she wants him, everybody else is supposed just step off? Please. Quincy wouldn't have anything to do with a woman with that kind of attitude, anyway," Karen said with certainty. "What you have to do, though, Lena, is step to her. Don't wait for her to corner you again, 'cause you know she's got more to say. So you set her straight, first!"

"Karen, I'm such a punk," Lena whined.

"Well, you're going to have to get tough, or people will step all over you. I promise you, Lena, if you go to her and let her know up front that she doesn't scare you, she'll leave you alone. She's a bully. Bullies are punks."

Lena didn't say anything immediately. She pondered Karen's words. "What if she doesn't back down?"

"She will."

"When do you think I should tell her?" Lena asked, but she already knew the answer.

"This afternoon," Karen said without hesitation.

When Lena got back to the office, it was difficult for her to concentrate on her normally simple job of answering the telephones and welcoming visitors. Karen's words rang repeatedly in her ears. Her stomach was in knots from just thinking about confronting Cheryl.

She knew she should do it that afternoon and get it over with, but she was genuinely afraid. She had never had a fight, and could barely remember any arguments she'd ever had. It was obvious to her that Cheryl had a potential for violence, and that was the last place she wanted to go.

The elevator bell rang seconds before the doors on the car closest to her opened. Out strolled Quincy. A broad smile automatically crossed her face and lit her eyes.

"Hi, there," he said with a sexy smile before

he was even near her desk. "How was lunch?" he asked as he stepped up to her.

"It was good."

"How's Karen?"

"She's good. She was talking about her pregnancy, mostly. She's really excited about it."

"I know. Serge is, too."

"He is? She doesn't think so."

"Believe me, he is."

"How was your lunch?"

"It was okay. I left them at the restaurant." Quincy had attended a luncheon being held for one of the department's employees who was retiring.

"I was going to ask you where everybody was."

"Yeah, they're getting wasted. I'm feeling a little tipsy myself, and I only had one drink. But you know what?"

"What?"

"You are so incredibly sexy." He leaned closer and whispered, "Do you know there's an iron rod in my pants?"

Lena couldn't help but blush.

"When I stepped off that elevator and got that first glimpse of you . . ." He shook his head and shrugged. "I have no control over it. It has a mind of its own."

Of course, they were alone in the reception area.

"If it can wait a couple of hours I'll talk to it later, and we can have a meeting of the minds," Lena said in a seductive whisper.

A chill passed though Quincy's body at her words. "You're not helping at all."He laughed.

She laughed, too.

"I love you," he said softly. "I'll talk to you later." He turned and walked back toward his office.

After Quincy had walked away, Lena sat there for the next few minutes with a smile on her face. *What a wonderful feeling it is to love someone so much, and to know that person loves you right back. Thank you, Quincy, for making me feel so much love from you. Thank you, God, for bringing him into my life.*

Lena picked up the telephone and dialed an extension. "Hi, Jen, it's Lena. Are you busy right now? Would you mind relieving me for a few minutes? I have to go to someone's office. Thank you."

I have to tell her now. There's no way I'm going to let her do anything to jeopardize my relationship with Quincy. God, give me strength.

Lena took a deep breath when she started down the hall to Cheryl's office. She realized that Karen *and* Quincy were right. She couldn't let anyone walk all over her. She had to put her foot down and be strong. After all, before Lena met Quincy she had been pretty much alone in the world. She didn't have anyone that she could call on when times got rough. A person had to be strong just to survive in this crazy world. Lena knew that if she needed to, she now had people she could call on, and she wanted to be there for them that way, as well. *Karen will be proud of me.*

When she reached Cheryl's office, she hesitated for a split second before she rapped lightly on the door.

At the same moment Quincy stepped out of his office, which was a few doors down from Cheryl's, and saw Lena at Cheryl's door. He called to her. She looked back at him briefly. Then she shook her head, waved him off, and disappeared into Cheryl's office.

"You got a minute, Cheryl? We need to talk," Lena said as she boldly entered Cheryl's office and closed the door. Her heart was racing once again.

"Yes, we do," Cheryl said, and she immediately rose from her chair.

"I want you to know that I don't appreciate you cornering me and attacking me about Quincy," Lena hurriedly began. She did not want to give Cheryl the upperhand.

"Oh, yeah? Well, I don't appreciate being stabbed in the back."

"When did I do that?"

"You told me you wasn't interested in him, and I told you I was. I told you if you was, I would step back, and that's what you shoulda done," Cheryl fired, immediately reverting to ghetto vernacular.

"Why, because that's what you say? Who said I have to follow your rules? First of all, I didn't go after Quincy. Quincy came after me. And why should I put him off? I can't help it if he likes me and not you."

"Look, let me tell you something." Cheryl pointed an accusatory finger at Lena. "You're messin' with the wrong person. I don't take

kindly to people backstabbin' me. I saw him
first, and I *will* have him whether you like it or
not, and if you try to get in my way you'll get
hurt. Do you understand me?"

"Don't threaten me!" Lena said with a force
that surprised her.

Cheryl too was surprised by the tone of Lena's
voice, but recovered quickly. "Whachu gonna'
do?"

Lena looked Cheryl straight in the eye and
said, "I don't want to fight you, Cheryl, but I'm
not going to let you step all over me like I'm
some idiot, either. I may not know as much
about men as you do, but I do know that Quincy
is my man, and I didn't have to hurt anyone to
get him. If you want to keep chasing after him
and trying to get him to pay attention to you,
believe me, the attention he pays you will not
be the attention you want.

"Now, I would appreciate it if you would leave
me and Quincy alone. Next time, I'll have him
come and talk to you, and I know he won't like
it—and neither will you—if I tell him you've
been threatening me." Lena turned and
opened the door. Suddenly, she had a last
thought and turned back. "Oh, and by the way,
I'm not a virgin." Then Lena proudly stepped
out of Cheryl's office.

Lena did not see the look of utter shock on
Cheryl's face, and she left the office too fast for
Cheryl to get in a retort. "Whew!" Lena said as
she hurried down the hall and back to her desk.
She wondered what Cheryl would do now.

She hadn't been back at her desk five minutes when Quincy called her.

"Hey, what were you doing in Cheryl's office?" he asked immediately.

"I needed to talk to her about something."

"May I ask what?"

"Well, basically about her harassing you and being rude to me," Lena said calmly.

"Really?"

"Yes."

Quincy smiled. "What brought this on?"

"Well, I didn't want to tell you, but she . . . I think she was going to start something with me yesterday. Someone walked in on us, so I made a hasty retreat," Lena admitted.

"When she came out of the rest room behind you."

"Yes."

"What did you tell her?" Quincy was tickled by Lena's sudden bravado.

"Well, Karen told me I had to make the first move, and just let her know that she can't walk all over me."

"I told you that, too."

"I know, but I didn't want you to know that I punked out yesterday. I was embarrassed."

"Angel, you don't ever have to be embarrassed about anything with me, okay?" he said tenderly. "I'm proud of you."

"Thank you, Quincy. I'm proud of me, too. I was scared, though."

"That's all right. There's nothing wrong with being afraid. It makes your senses sharper."

"I wonder if she's going to bother me again.

I didn't really give her a chance to get the last word in."

"You're not supposed to. I doubt if she'll mess with you anymore though. She knows now that you're not going to stand for it."

"Yeah, and I also threatened her with you."

TWENTY

Summer seemed to come early. On Friday of the Memorial Day weekend, the mercury rose to ninety-five degrees. Temperatures ranging in the high nineties were forecast for the entire weekend.

Quincy's parents lived in a two-family home in the Bedford-Stuyvesant section of Brooklyn, the house where Quincy had grown up. When he and his siblings were children, the Taylor family occupied the entire house. It was not until all of the children were grown and on their own that Quincy's father had the house converted into a two-family as an extra source of income. Currently, Quincy's younger brother, Aaron, his wife, Linda, and their two daughters rented the second apartment.

Since the weather was expected to be so beautiful for the entire weekend, Quincy's parents decided to throw a backyard barbecue. Lena was excited about the prospect of meeting them, and his sisters and brothers.

Lena did not want to get too dressy because it was a cookout, but she wanted to look especially nice for her first meeting with Quincy's family. Quincy thought she was making too much of the whole thing, and tried to convince her that she did not have to go to any extremes.

"Just be yourself, angel, and they can't help but love you," Quincy told her.

Nevertheless, Lena decided on a cool, light-weight, pale pink, cotton dress. It was sleeveless with a scoop neck in front, and cinched at the waist by darts. The dress was midi length, and one of Lena's own designs.

Serge and Karen arrived at the Taylor house at the same time as Quincy and Lena.

"Hi, Karen," Lena called when she stepped out of the car.

"Hi, Lena." The women walked toward each other and embraced. "How're you feeling? I love this dress, Lena. Did you make it?"

"Yes."

"It's gorgeous. I'd love for you to make me something. I'll pay whatever you ask, too."

"I'll make you a maternity outfit," Lena volunteered.

"You will?"

"Sure."

"Thank you."

"Hi, Lena," Serge called.

She turned in his direction. "Hi, Serge. How you doin'?"

"I'm good. How're you?"

"Good."

"What's up, man?" Serge greeted Quincy. They shook hands and embraced.

"What's up, dude? How you doin'?"

"I'm cool."

"Hey, Karen," Quincy said. He stepped over to Karen and Lena and kissed Karen's cheek.

"Hi, Q. How you doing, hon?"

"I'm good. How *you* doin'?" he asked, and rubbed her belly.

She giggled and said, "I'm fine."

Quincy led them straight to the backyard. His father was at the grill. He wore an apron that read simply COOK. Lena was amazed; Quincy was the spitting image of his father.

"Hey, Pop. What's up?" Quincy asked as he stepped over to his father and kissed his cheek.

"Hey, Q, how you doin', man? The ribs are gonna be better than ever this year. I've improved my sauce," Mr. Taylor said.

"You say that every year."

"Well, this is it, this time." Mr. Taylor turned his attention to Lena. "Is this the young lady you were telling me about, Q?"

"Yeah, Pop. This is Lena Caldwell," Quincy said tenderly as he reached for her hand.

"Hello, Lena," Mr. Taylor said as he removed the cooking mitt from his hand and reached out to shake hers.

Lena took his hand firmly, and with a big smile said, "Hi, Mr. Taylor. I'm so happy to meet you."

"Well, the pleasure's all mine, Miss Lena," Mr. Taylor said, laying on the charm. He gave Quincy a look of approval.

Quincy beamed.

Mr. Taylor then greeted Karen and Serge.

"Where's Mom?" Quincy asked his father.

"She's in the house."

"Come on, angel. I want you to meet my mother." Quincy took her hand and led her to the back door.

"Hi, baby," his mother said as she suddenly came through the back door. She was carrying a big bowl of salad.

"Hi, Mom," Quincy said as he kissed her. "Give me that." He took the bowl from her hands and placed it on the table closest to them. He turned back to her and said, "Mom, this is Lena Caldwell. Lena, this is my mom."

"Hi, Mrs. Taylor," Lena said, then embraced her and kissed her cheek.

"Hello, Lena. It's so nice to meet you. I've heard so much about you. I don't know what took Quincy so long in bringing you over so we could meet," Mrs. Taylor said as she cut her eyes at Quincy.

"It's nice to meet you, too. I've been looking forward to this day."

"Well, you come on in and make yourself right at home. Would you like something to drink, honey?" Mrs. Taylor asked Lena.

"Oh, no thank you, Mrs. Taylor. I'm fine for now."

"Okay. Hi, Serge and Karen," Mrs. Taylor said, and she embraced them both. "How're you both doing?"

"We're fine, Mom," Serge said. "How you doin'?"

"I'm doing just fine. I'm so happy you came. And congratulations are in order, I understand," Mrs. Taylor said suddenly.

"Oh, yes, thank you," Karen said.

"So when's the wedding, Serge?" his "other mother" asked.

Karen looked up at Serge expectantly, eager to hear how he was going to answer.

"We haven't set a date yet, but it'll be soon. Before the baby gets here, anyway," Serge said.

Karen's expression changed. Her eyes watered suddenly, because she knew he would never tell Quincy's mother a lie. Serge looked over at her. He took her hand and kissed her softly on her neck.

Before the day was over, Lena had met so many people that it made her head spin. She met all four of his brothers and their wives and children, three of his four sisters and their husbands or significant others, their children, and numerous relatives and friends of the family. There was an enormous turnout. They did not leave to return home until close to eleven o'clock that night. They had arrived at one that afternoon.

Lena had the time of her life. She had never laughed so much as she did in that one day with Quincy's family. Everyone was wonderful, and welcomed her with open arms. And it was obvious that everyone knew Quincy was in love. No one was surprised to meet her.

Over the Fourth of July holiday, Quincy, Lena, Karen, and Serge took a trip to Virginia Beach. That was quite an experience for Lena. She was in total disbelief the first time the four of them walked down the main strip off the beach in

search of a restaurant in which they could have
dinner. Young women clad in nearly nothing at
all paraded up and down the street, flirting
shamelessly with young men who obviously had
highly inflamed libidos.

"Can they walk around like that? That's not
against the law?" Lena whispered urgently to
Quincy as they moved along the crowded side-
walk.

"No, angel, it's not against the law. It should
be, right?"

"Yes! If I had a daughter and she was walking
up and down the street like these young girls,
I'd yank her butt up so fast she wouldn't know
what hit her."

"I heard that."

Despite how much she disliked the lewdness
of the strip, Lena enjoyed her weekend with
Quincy. She did not know how to swim, but before they checked out of the hotel at the end
of their three-day stay, Lena could float, dog
paddle, and swim underwater.

At the end of July, Quincy bought Lena a bi-
cycle. He often rode with his friends, usually taking long trips upstate, but now he wanted to
share the time he expended cycling with Lena.

Biking had always been one of Lena's joys. It
was the one activity that her parents never lim-
ited because they liked to ride, also.

Lena kept her bike at Quincy's apartment because, most often, they rode around Prospect
Park. They got up first thing in the morning
and rode around the park a few times before
they started their day. Lena loved spending the

early hours with him, communing with nature as they breezed through the park at a steady pace.

Quincy and Lena grew closer and closer with each new day. Despite the fact that they worked together and slept together practically every night, they never tired of each other. They talked about everything, and Lena had an eagerness to catch up with everyone else, so she always had questions for him. Quincy, ever patient, encouraged her to ask him anything she wanted to know. He never lied to her, either; if he didn't know the answer, he said so.

By the middle of September, Lena and Quincy were inseparable. They had exchanged keys to each other's homes and spent every night together, without exception, either in Brooklyn or in the Bronx.

Their relationship blossomed into a very special one. Not only were they lovers, but friends as well. They were so comfortable with each other that they were able to be completely honest about everything. Although they spent most of their free time together, they also each participated in activities apart from one another.

As their love blossomed, Lena seemed to blossom, too. She and Karen had quickly become friends, and they began to spend a lot of time together apart from Quincy and Serge. Lena had also enrolled in college to resume her pursuit of a degree. She became much more outspoken as the months passed, especially after her ordeal with Cheryl, and many times Quincy jokingly reminded her of how timid she had been when they first met.

Almost by accident, Lena began to sew professionally as a sideline. As promised, she made the maternity outfit for Karen, who seemed to get bigger and bigger with each passing day. The outfit was a three-piece suit: a long jacket which she could wear after she had the baby by simply cinching the waist with a belt, a skirt with an elasticized waistband, and wide-legged drawstring pants. Karen was so delighted with the suit, and so amazed that Lena had been able to complete the whole thing in less than two weeks, that she suggested Lena do seamstress work on the side for extra money. Lena had never even considered sewing for money before, but with a little coaxing from Karen, Quincy, and Serge, she decided to give it a shot.

As a result of her new sideline, Lena began to meet more people and make new friends. Quincy loved the change in her. Her confidence grew, and with it she matured into an even more beautiful woman than she had been when he first laid eyes on her.

During the first week of September, Quincy treated Lena to a four-day trip to Cancun, Mexico, for her birthday, which fell on September third. It was the first time Lena had ever been out of the country. Many times over the summer, they had wanted to go away for an entire week, but Quincy had not accrued vacation time yet. Now, since she was going back to school and her classes were scheduled to start right after Labor Day, they were forced to put vacation plans on hold. During their Cancun trip, although Quincy did not actually propose to Lena, they discussed marriage and the prospect of having a family together.

At the bank, they usually ate lunch together every day, and—although they were quite subdued around the office—it was no secret that they were an item. Due to his managerial position, Quincy made a point of not spending too much time at the reception desk with Lena, but they spoke on the telephone at least two or three times a day.

Lena was enrolled in an accounting class on Tuesday evenings from six to nine and a sociology class on Thursday evenings from six-thirty to nine-thirty. Since her school was located in lower Manhattan, on those nights she stayed in Brooklyn with Quincy so she would not have to travel all the way to the Bronx that late by herself.

Quincy was very athletic, and still spent many evenings after work playing some type of sport—basketball, softball, or racquetball. Although they spent every night together, many times from five to nine-thirty or ten o'clock, as a result of Lena's classes and Quincy's hobbies, they were often apart. Nonetheless, both always valued the time they spent together.

TWENTY-ONE

It was a very warm Thursday afternoon in early October. Quincy and Lena had lunch in an outdoor café and were feeling very amorous when they strolled back to the office.

When they stepped off the elevator, Lena hinted about sharing a bath with him later that evening, and Quincy's response was, "You bring the bubbles, I'll supply the water."

As Lena was about to step behind her desk, Quincy glanced around quickly to be sure no one was watching and then pinched her on her backside.

"See you later, sweet cheeks," he said with a flirtatious grin.

"You can count on it," was her reply.

At approximately three-thirty that afternoon, as Lena sat at her desk sorting through her files, she looked up and noticed a strikingly beautiful black woman stepping off the elevator. She was tall—Lena figured she had to be at least six feet—and very slim without being skinny. Her complexion was a golden brown as if she were tanned, and her hair was cut short in a pixie style with soft brown curls shadowing her forehead. She wore a long, deep purple, V-neck coat with gold buttons and a matching, midi-length, straight skirt with a front side slit that started just above her knee. Her jewelry consisted of a very ornate gold necklace with matching earrings and bracelet.

Lena thought she was quite graceful. The woman seemed to glide from the elevator to her desk. When she reached the desk, Lena noticed that her makeup was flawless and her smile brilliant.

"Good afternoon," Lena said pleasantly. "May I help you?"

"Yes. Good afternoon," the woman said. "I'm here to see Quincy Taylor. My name is Rhonda Clark."

"All right, Ms. Clark. If you'll have a seat I'll let him know you're here."

"Thank you," she said graciously, and turned to have a seat in the reception area.

Lena picked up her telephone and dialed Quincy's extension.

"Quincy Taylor," he announced when he picked up the telephone.

"Hi. There's a woman named Rhonda Clark here to see you," she told him.

There was a pregnant pause before he asked, "Who?"

"Rhonda Clark," Lena repeated. She did not notice the distress in his voice.

Quincy was silent on the line for a few seconds, which prompted Lena to ask, "Did you hear me?"

"Huh? Oh, yeah."

"What's the matter?" she asked in a whisper.

"Nothing. I'll be right out," he said, and he abruptly hung up the phone.

Lena frowned briefly, wondering why he'd sounded so strange. She turned to Ms. Clark, however, and said, "He'll be right with you."

"Thank you."

Meanwhile, Quincy sat at his desk in a state of panic. His heart was beating at a phenomenal rate, and suddenly his palms felt very sweaty.

What is Rhonda doing here? When did she get back? He had finally forgotten about her, completely wiped her from his memory, and now she was back. *For what?* he wondered. He took a deep breath and rose from his seat slowly, trying to gather the courage to walk out to the reception area to greet her.

He was standing just inside his door, seemingly unable to move, when Maritza entered his office. "What's the matter?" she asked with concern when she saw his pain-stricken face.

"Huh? Oh, nothing. I was just thinking about something," he said blankly.

"You sure?"

"Yeah. Listen, there's a woman in the reception area for me. Could you go get her and bring her back?"

"I didn't know you had an appointment this afternoon."

"I don't. She's an unexpected visitor. Her name's Rhonda Clark."

"Okay. I'll be right back."

"Thanks, Maritza."

Quincy was nervous about seeing Rhonda. It had been almost two years since she moved to

Los Angeles. She had never written or called. He wondered why she was here now. *What does she want with me?*

He strolled across the office and gazed out the window. He did not want to see Rhonda. All he could think about was the way she had left him.

"Here we are," he heard Maritza say cheerfully behind his back.

He turned to them. He looked past Rhonda and spoke to Maritza. "Would you close the door, please, Maritza?"

"Sure," she answered as she pulled the door closed behind her.

Rhonda smiled warily and said, "Hello, Quincy."

He stared at her for a few seconds, his face giving away no trace of the panic that filled his heart. "What are you doing here?" he finally asked.

"I wanted to see you. How have you been?"

"What difference does it make to you?"

Rhonda's lip quivered involuntarily. "I don't blame you for hating me, Quincy, but I had to see you. I've been home for almost two months now, and I've been trying to find the courage to call you."

He turned his back to her. He felt his emotions slipping, and did not want to show her any signs of weakness. He had noticed, though, that she looked beautiful, even more beautiful than when she left two years ago. He wondered why she was back, but did not want to ask for fear she would think he cared.

His tongue seemed to operate independently from his brain, because he heard himself ask, "Why did you come back?" His back was still to her.

"The job fell through. Ray Nestor turned out to be a real creep. I didn't find out until I was out there that there were conditions to getting the layout," she explained.

Rhonda was a professional model. She'd left him two years ago, when she was offered a high-profile photo layout by one of the country's top photographers. The only problem was that she had to move to Los Angeles. They had been together for three and a half years, had been engaged for four months when she left. Rhonda had been immovable and uncompromising in her decision to leave. She claimed it was the chance of a lifetime for her. It had not mattered that her leaving tore his heart in two.

When Quincy did not respond, Rhonda continued. "I tried to get other modeling jobs while I was out there, but none of them amounted to anything. It was almost as if he had blackballed me. I took some really crappy jobs just to pay my bills. I was working as a waitress before I left." She took a couple of steps toward him. "I missed you, Quincy."

"Did you really?" he asked as he turned sharply to face her. "You never called me. You never wrote me. Is that how much you missed me?"

"I know. I'm sorry."

"You're sorry? What do you want from me? What did you think? That I'd be sitting here waiting for you? You hurt me, Rhonda. You didn't care about me! You didn't care what I felt! All you cared about was some promise that slimeball made you about making you this great star," he said nastily. "He didn't give a damn about you. I did! And you left me without a second thought."

His words tore at her heart. She had expected him to be angry, but she could not stand knowing that he despised her the way he obviously did. She could not stop the tears from falling, and, although she tried to choke back a sob, she was unsuccessful.

"I'm sorry, Quincy. I didn't mean to hurt you. I thought about you every day I was there," Rhonda cried. "I'm so sorry."

"I never did anything to hurt you. I was always there for you, and you walked out on me. Do you know how that made me feel? Do you know what you did to me when you left?"

Rhonda felt totally ashamed of herself. He was right, too. He had always been there for her, always treated her like royalty. But at the time, she'd felt that she was doing the right thing, that she had to take that chance. If she hadn't, she would have spent the rest of her life wondering what if?

Rhonda had known that he would not be happy to see her, but she had hoped against hope that he had missed her just a little bit and would be glad to see that she was all right. She could see now that she had been mistaken.

She pulled a frilly handkerchief from her purse and began to gently dab the tears from her eyes. "I'm sorry, Quincy," she said as she tried to compose herself. "I should have never come here. I won't bother you again."

She turned toward the door to leave.

Quincy stood where he was and watched as she started to leave. Her hand was on the doorknob when, against his will, he called out, "Rhonda, wait."

He took a tentative step toward her and she slowly turned back to him.

When she looked into his eyes she saw the tears that threatened to fall, and she knew that he still cared for her. She crossed the room in what seemed like one giant step and threw her arms around him.

Before Quincy realized what he was doing he was embracing her, and he held her tight as his tears fell, uninhibited. It was almost as if someone else had taken over his mind and body. She felt good in his arms, the way she used to.

"I love you, Quincy," he heard her cry. "I love you so much, and I'm so sorry for hurting you. Please, forgive me?"

Quincy could not answer. He was so glad to see her and hold her again. He had missed her so much that he could not begin to explain it. She had been his whole life. She had been everything to him.

"Rhonda." He sighed.

"I missed you so much. I thought about you every day."

"I missed you, too. Why didn't you call me?"

"I was afraid to. I knew how angry you were,

and I hated thinking that you didn't love me anymore," Rhonda explained.

"How could you think that I didn't love you?"

"I don't know." She lowered her head in shame as they moved apart.

"Stop crying," he said gently as he reached up to wipe a tear from her eye.

As she tried to catch her breath, she cracked a nervous smile and said, "It's so good to see you. You look great."

"So do you," he said softly. Then, as if he had just noticed, he said, "You cut your hair."

"Yeah. Just before I left."

They stood in the middle of his office staring at one another. There were so many things they both wanted to say, but neither really knew where to start.

Quincy slowly moved over to his desk. "Where are you staying?" he asked.

"With my mother."

He looked at his watch and said, "I have a meeting in about ten minutes."

"All right."

"Do you want to have dinner?"

"I'd love to," she said with a bright smile.

"I should be leaving here about six or six-thirty. Will you be home?"

"Yes. Do you still have my mother's address?"

"How could I forget it?"

She smiled softly at him.

"I'll pick you up about seven?"

"All right," she answered.

He stepped away from his desk then, and said, "Come on. I'll walk you out."

Lena was speaking with a visitor of the bank when Quincy and Rhonda passed through the reception area. From the corner of her eye she noticed that he embraced Rhonda before she got on the elevator.

When Quincy came back past her desk she asked, "Who was that?"

"An old friend that just moved back into town," he answered solemnly.

When he did not stop, she asked, "Quincy, what's wrong?"

He turned back to her and answered, "Nothing. I have a meeting to go to. I'll talk to you later."

He continued through the reception area without another word to her. Lena had gotten a very unsettling feeling in her stomach when she looked into his eyes. It seemed as if he did not want to face her. She wondered why.

Quincy knew Lena would be leaving the office no later than five-thirty because she had classes that evening. When she came back to his office at five o'clock, he lied and told her he would probably be there until six because he had a late meeting with his boss. He knew he could not tell her he was going to see Rhonda when he left. He hated lying to her, but with his feelings all jumbled up the way they were at the moment he felt he had no other alternative.

As much as he hated to admit it, especially to himself, he was glad Rhonda was back. She looked great, and he actually looked forward to seeing her that night.

When Quincy left the office at five forty-five,

he went home and picked up his car. Rhonda's mother lived in Manhattan, and on the drive from Brooklyn he tried to reconcile his thoughts about her return. He wondered if she was really there to stay, or if there was a possibility of her running out on him again.

Quincy wondered why she had taken so long to get in touch with him. She said she had been back for two months. He could not forget the effect her leaving had on him. He had been devastated. Two years ago, she was his whole life.

They had been seeing each other for three years when he asked her to marry him. He had been very nervous about asking her. Although she had always told him how much she loved him, he had always felt that there were limits to her love. Quincy, who would have done anything she asked and often did, had thought Rhonda would be hesitant to commit to him for life. He could remember how happy he had been when she said yes.

It was Valentine's Day, and he had taken her to her favorite French restaurant, although he was not particularly fond of French food. He bought her a dozen, long-stemmed, red roses. He ordered a bottle of Moet & Chandon champagne. As they were waiting for their dessert, he presented her with a one and a half carat diamond ring that he had not even finished paying for.

Quincy could remember it as if it were yesterday. She began to cry, and told him that she would love him for as long as she lived. Then she said yes.

The memory of that day and the day she left him fought for prominence in his mind. How could he ignore the way she'd left? He knew he couldn't. But she was back now, and that was all that mattered at the moment.

When Quincy picked her up from her mother's house that evening, Rhonda had changed her clothes and was wearing a short leather jacket and jeans. She looked as beautiful as ever.

Once they were in his car and on their way, Quincy said softly without looking at her, "I've missed you, Rhonda."

"I've missed you, too," she whispered.

"How long are you home for?"

"Forever."

He looked over at her to see if she was being sincere, then turned his attention back to the road.

She reached over and touched his hand. "I won't leave you anymore, Quincy."

They had dinner in a quiet little café in the Village. She told him about all the things that had gone wrong for her while she was in California. He refused to tell her about how hard it had been for him when she left, other than to say how much it had hurt him. They sat close together in the restaurant, nursed a bottle of wine long after they had finished eating, and talked. When they finally left the restaurant, they went to the movies. After the movie, they strolled around in the Village for over an hour, holding hands and just being together.

Quincy did not mention anything about Lena,

although thoughts of her flashed through his mind constantly while he was with Rhonda. He felt guilty for not telling Rhonda the truth, but he was being selfish. All Quincy knew was how he felt being with her again, and he did not want that feeling to end.

It was well after midnight when they finally made their way back to where he had parked his car. They stood against his car wrapped in an embrace like a couple of teenagers, not really saying much but just being close. Quincy could not deny how much he wanted to make love to her; it was, of course, a purely emotional feeling over which he had no control. Rhonda, too, was feeling quite lustful; she had not been with a man in almost a year.

"Take me home with you, Quincy," she sighed in his ear. "I want to make love with you."

Quincy did not answer her immediately. He knew he would have to tell her about Lena now, though.

"Quincy?"

He pushed her away suddenly.

"What's the matter?" she wanted to know.

"We can't go to my house."

"Why not?"

He lowered his head and told her, "There's someone there."

Rhonda felt as though she had been slapped. *What did you expect?* she asked herself. *You've been gone for two years.* "I'm sorry," she said softly. "I don't know why I thought you'd be here waiting for me to come back."

Quincy did not respond.

"Is it serious?" she asked.

"Yes."

He looked into her eyes, then, and could see tears straining to fall. He reached up and caressed her face. "Don't cry."

She reached for him and hugged him close once more. "I love you, Quincy. I still love you."

When Lena arrived at Quincy's house that night, it was ten-thirty. She was surprised when she opened the door and found all of the lights out. *Could he be in bed this early?* she wondered.

"Quincy!"

She turned on the living room light and started to remove her jacket. She tossed it on the couch and then walked back to the bedroom, calling for him again. "Quincy."

When she turned on the bedroom light she saw that the bed was still made, and there were no signs that he had even been there. She wondered where he was.

She walked back to the living room, picked her jacket up from the couch, and hung it in the closet. Then she went to the kitchen and opened the refrigerator to see what she could grab to eat. There were spaghetti and meatballs leftover from Tuesday. She decided to warm some up for dinner.

While the food was warming, she returned to the bedroom to get undressed. She put on one of his pajama tops and her fluffy slippers, then returned to the kitchen to check on her food. When she saw that it was not quite ready, she went into the living room and turned on the television. She sat and watched the last ten minutes of *ER*.

As she ate her dinner she watched the late news, and when that went off she watched *The Tonight Show* until she became too tired to keep her eyes open. When she noticed the time, it was twelve-ten. As she got up to turn the television off so she could go to bed, she wondered again where Quincy was. *He could have at least left a message on the answering machine,* she thought as she tucked herself into bed.

Once in bed, she could not get to sleep, although she had been nodding off just minutes before. Her thoughts returned to the strange way Quincy had acted that afternoon at work. He'd told her that the woman, Rhonda Clark, was an old friend who had just returned to town, but the more she thought about it the more she realized that his strange behavior began the moment she let him know Rhonda Clark was there to see him. Lena could not help but wonder if there was more to his friendship with the woman than he had let on.

She was not sure what time it was when she finally fell off to sleep, but at four thirty-five when she awoke to go to the bathroom Quincy still was not home. When she returned to the bed, her mind was working overtime, trying to figure out what was going on with him. He had never behaved this way before. He had never gone out and not told her where he was going or when he would be returning, and it was not

like him to not have called. He had to know
that she would be worried about him.

Lena lay there for the next half an hour making excuses for Quincy, surmising that there had
to be a reasonable and logical explanation for
his staying out all night without calling. Just
then, she heard his keys in the door. Her body
stiffened for a moment, and she looked over at
the clock radio on his nightstand. 5:10 A.M. Initially, she considered pretending that she was
asleep, but there were too many questions burn-
ing in her mind. She decided to confront him.
She had to know what was going on.

After dropping Rhonda off at her mother's
house, Quincy had driven home slowly. He was
not looking forward to telling Lena why he was
so late. He had already decided that he would
not lie to her. She deserved to know the truth.
He pulled into the parking garage in his building at four forty-five. He sat in his car for the
next twenty minutes trying to decide how to tell
her about Rhonda.

He knew there was no way he could spare her
the heartbreak of his truth. He knew how she
felt about him and, in all honesty, he loved
Lena, too. He felt undeserving of her love, however, especially after spending the entire night
with Rhonda.

When he finally accepted the fact that he
could no longer prolong the inevitable, he got
out of his car and lumbered over to the elevator.
Thoughts of Rhonda filled his head. He could
still smell her perfume. He did not want to hurt

Lena, but he felt as if his back were against the wall.

He unlocked the door to his apartment and stepped into the darkness of his living room. He did not bother to turn on the light as he removed his trench coat and hung it in the closet. He placed his keys on the coffee table as he passed it, and walked slowly back to his room. When he entered it he did not bother to turn on those lights, either. He stood at his closet as he removed his suit jacket and pulled a hanger from the rod and hung it there. His tie hung loosely around his neck, and his shirt collar was opened. After a few seconds, he moved over to the bed and sat there with his back to Lena. He never once looked over at her, and was stunned when her voice cut through the darkness.

"Where have you been?"

He turned to her, surprised that she was not asleep. Even in the darkness he could see the tears in her eyes. As he turned back around he suddenly felt very ashamed of what he had done.

"I was with Rhonda," he said barely above a whisper.

"You were where?" she asked. He had spoken so softly that she did not hear him.

"I was with Rhonda," he repeated, a decibel or two louder.

"Who is . . . ? That woman who came to the bank yesterday?"

"Yes."

Lena continued to lie where she was, but a tear rolled down the side of her face into her ear as the realization of what he said hit her. She suddenly felt as if she couldn't breathe.

After what seemed like minutes, she asked, "Who is she?" Her voice was quavering because she really hadn't wanted to ask him that; she was too afraid of what his answer might be.

Quincy sighed and lowered his head. He did not answer her right away, so she had no choice but to ask him again—this time with more force. "Who is she!"

"She was my fiancée."

"Your fiancée!" Lena cried. That was the last thing she'd expected to hear. She stared at him in disbelief through the darkness of the room, tears falling unbidden from her eyes.

He turned back to her, then. Quincy's heart ached from knowing how he had hurt her, was hurting her, but he had to tell her the truth. He realized then that he should have told her about Rhonda a long time ago.

He began to explain. "I'm sorry that I didn't tell you before, Lena. I know now that I should have. You deserved to know about her, and about me, from the beginning. I was engaged to her two and a half years ago. She was a fashion model, and about four months before our scheduled wedding she got an offer for a job with this big-time photographer. The only thing was, in order for her to get the job she had to move to LA. She called off our wedding, and told me that it was the chance of a lifetime for her. She left me."

By this time, Quincy was close to tears. His voice trembled as he continued his story.

"I tried to talk her out of going, but nothing I said seemed to matter to her. When she left . . . I was devastated when she left." He turned his back to her once more and looked down at his hands as he spoke; he was too ashamed to face Lena. "I thought I had finally gotten her out of my system," he continued. "When she showed up at the office yesterday, at first I was angry. But for some reason, I couldn't . . . I was glad that she came back."

Once again she had to ask him a question she wasn't sure she wanted the answer to. "You still love her, don't you?" Lena asked. As she lay frozen in place with tears endlessly streaming from her eyes, she tried to steel herself against what his answer might be.

"I don't know, Lena. I don't know what I'm feeling right now. I'm sorry. I don't want to hurt you. That's the last thing I want to do. I love you, but I've got all these feelings turning around inside of me, and I don't know what to do," he lamented.

Lena lay there for a moment and tried to digest his words. Her heart was breaking, and she feared that she would lose him to this woman he had loved so strongly two years ago.

Suddenly, she sat up on the bed. Tears steadily poured out of her eyes, and try as she might she could not quell them.

"I love you, Quincy," she sobbed.

He felt terrible knowing that he had hurt her. She did not deserve that. He rose from the bed and walked around to her side.

"I'm sorry, Lena. I'm so sorry."

Lena rose from the bed, but Quincy mistook her intentions. When he reached out to embrace her, she moved away from him and pulled her arm out of his grasp.

"No. Don't touch me."

She walked past him and out of the room. She went into the living room and sat on the sofa. Rocking back and forth, she wrapped her arms around herself and cried out her pain.

Quincy could hear her cries from the bedroom, and the sound cut him in two. After listening to her for nearly five minutes, he followed her into the other room. He knelt before her and tried to soothe her aching heart, but the more he tried she only seemed to cry harder.

Lena was feeling pitiful. Suddenly her life before Quincy loomed in front of her, and she began to feel as if her whole relationship with him had been a horrible trick that some unforeseen puppet-master had played on her, and she was about to be flung back into her real world of loneliness. "You might as well go back to her," Lena moaned between sobs, self-pity overwhelming her.

"Lena, please don't cry."

"Go on! You know you still love her! Go to her! I don't want you to stay with me if you're just doing it because you feel sorry for me!" she cried. "You said you don't know what you're feeling. Well, the only way for you to find out is if you go back to her."

"Lena, don't push me away. Please. Don't push me away."

"I don't want you if you're not even sure how you feel about her or me."

He rose from his knee to sit beside her on the sofa and tried to embrace her, but she fought him off.

"No, leave me alone! Just leave me alone."

"Lena, I love you," Quincy implored.

"Don't tell me you love me and then tell me in the next breath that you're not sure if you still love her," Lena replied angrily. "You can't have it both ways, Quincy! You have to make a choice. Until you do, I want you to leave me alone!"

He knew she was right. In his heart Quincy knew he would have to make a choice. He had invested so many years of his life in his relationship with Rhonda. Now that she was back, he almost felt as though he owed it to himself to finally reap some benefits from all of the love he had so unselfishly given her. But with Lena, he had to take into account that the time they shared had been sheer perfection, although they had only been together for several months. There was no guesswork in loving her. She was open and honest, naturally so. She did not know about pretense; she was sincere to the point of naiveté.

Lena rose abruptly from the sofa and stormed into the bathroom. She slammed the door and locked it behind her. Quincy hung his head in shame.

This was all new to her. Lena had never been in love before she met Quincy, so she had never experienced the pain of a broken heart. It was unbearable.

As she stood at his sink with a facecloth in hand, trying to wipe the tears from her eyes, she studied her reflection and hated what she saw. *How could he do this to me,* she asked herself, *if he really loves me like he said? How could he even think about being with anyone else?* It did not matter to her that he had once loved this woman Rhonda. What mattered was that she had left him and had broken his heart. Quincy had to know what she was feeling now. How could he want to inflict that kind of pain on her, knowing firsthand what it was like?

Twenty minutes passed before she was finally able to stem the flow of her tears. She considered taking the day off from work, but decided to go in, anyway. She knew she would spend the entire day crying over Quincy if she did not keep herself busy.

She turned on the shower and adjusted the water until it was good and hot. She removed the pajama top she was wearing and her panties and stepped under the spray. As the water poured over her body, she tried to block him out of her mind. She did not want to think about Quincy or his fiancée. Try as she might, though, all she could see was them together.

During the twenty-five minutes that she was in the shower, Lena decided that, for her own piece of mind, she would go straight home when she got off from work that evening. She also decided to give him back his keys. As long as he was not sure who he was in love with or wanted to be with, there was no way she would be coming back there.

When she got out of the shower and returned to the bedroom, Quincy was sitting on his bed looking pitiful. She tried to ignore him as she went about getting her clothes ready for work.

"Lena."

"What?"

"Please don't be angry with me."

"I'm not angry with you, Quincy. I'm just . . . I'm hurt, and I'm disappointed. But what difference does it make? You have to do what you have to do."

"You're going to work?"

"Yes."

"I'm gonna take the day off today. I need to get some sleep," he said.

"Yeah, I'm sure you're exhausted," she said sarcastically.

Just then, Lena, clad only in her panties and bra, walked out of the bedroom and into the living room to retrieve her pocketbook. She removed her key ring and unfastened the clasp and pulled off the three keys he had given her to his apartment. She strode back to his bedroom and stepped directly in front of him with her hand out.

"Here. Take your keys."

Quincy looked up at her, and she could not ignore the poignant sadness in his eyes. But she could not let that move her. He had brought this all on himself.

"Lena, don't . . ." He stopped himself in mid-sentence. He realized how unfair and selfish it would be of him to expect her to take this all with a grain of salt. He reached out and took the keys from her hand.

"Can I have my keys, please?" she said in a quavering voice.

Quincy looked into her eyes again, pleading silently with her to forgive him. When he had not moved after a few minutes, Lena said, "Quincy, I want my keys."

Knowing he had no right to ask her for anything, Quincy slowly rose from the bed and lumbered out to the living room. He picked up his key ring from the table and stared at it for a few seconds. Tears clouded his eyes as he slowly removed Lena's keys from the ring. Angrily, he threw the remaining keys on the couch and turned to go back to his room, but Lena was right behind him. He stretched out his hand to give her the keys, and when she reached for them he grabbed her hand and held it. "Lena, I do love you. I swear I do."

She couldn't stand to see him cry, but she pulled her hand away and turned to walk back to the bedroom to finish getting dressed.

By the time she had ironed her clothes and was fully dressed and ready to get out of there, it was only seven-thirty. She felt drained already. She did not have to report to work until eight-thirty, and from Quincy's place the trip only took twenty minutes. She did not want to go in that early, but she certainly did not want to hang around looking at a pitiful Quincy, so she left.

TWENTY-TWO

Although she tried with all her might, Lena was not able to disguise the anguish that filled her heart. On most days she was uncommonly cheerful, with a smile and a pleasant word for everyone. On this particular Friday, concerned coworkers inquired all morning as to what it was that was bothering her, because her smile was gone and her eyes were sad and swollen from crying.

About a half an hour before she was scheduled to go to lunch, Lena telephoned Karen. She felt she had to talk to someone, and she knew that Karen would probably know all about this woman Rhonda that Quincy seemed to be so in love with.

While they were on the phone, Karen could tell from the tone of Lena's voice that there was something wrong. Although Karen asked her repeatedly what it was, Lena would not say. Karen got the impression that Lena was pleading with her to meet for lunch. Since they worked only a few blocks away from each other, Karen promised to meet her in front of her office at one o'clock.

At twenty to one, Lena called Sarah, one of

the secretaries who sat closest to the reception area, and asked her to cover the front desk for five minutes while she went to the ladies' room. When she stepped into the bathroom, there were two women standing at the sink talking. They both said hello to her and asked if she were okay, for they had noticed that she looked a bit sad. Lena put on a false smile, which looked more like a grimace of pain, and assured them that she was all right.

As she sat in the stall, her thoughts once again drifted back to Quincy and Rhonda. She began to cry softly. She sat there for almost five minutes until she realized that she was abusing Sarah's kindness by sitting there brooding.

When she stepped out of the stall, Cheryl Stewart was standing at the mirror, touching up her makeup.

"Hi, Lena," she said, pleasantly.

"Hi."

Following their altercation earlier in the year, Cheryl had developed a new respect for Lena. Cheryl admired the way Lena had spoken up for herself, challenging her to try to woo Quincy. Once she had gotten over the initial shock of Lena's boldness, she had apologized. Cheryl admitted that she had been way out of line. Before their conversation ended, the girls had even laughed together about how Lena had immediately taken the defensive when Cheryl approached her, as if gearing up to go at it with her again. Since that time, whenever they saw each other Cheryl had gone out of her way to speak to Lena, always in a polite manner and always with a warm smile.

Cheryl noticed that Lena was purposely trying to avoid looking in her direction.

"You all right?" Cheryl asked with genuine concern.

"Uh-huh," Lena mumbled.

Lena tried hard to remain composed. She really did not want to break down in front of Cheryl. To her dismay, her eyes welled up and spilled over. She hastily brushed the tears from her face, and tried to cover the movement by quickly blowing her nose.

Cheryl closed her makeup compact and turned to Lena. "What's the matter?"

"Nothing," Lena said, unable to stifle her sobs.

Cheryl moved closer to her and placed a hand on her shoulder. "Hey, come on. What's wrong, Lena?" she asked. "Did you and Quincy have a fight?"

Lena shook her head "no" as her sobs became stronger and louder.

Seeing how overwrought she had become, Cheryl put her arms around her and tried to comfort her. "Oh, honey. You guys didn't break up, did you?"

Lena tried to catch her breath as she looked at Cheryl through tear-filled eyes.

"I don't know," she moaned. "He came home at five o'clock this morning and told me that he was with this woman who used to be his fiancée. They were engaged, and she broke up with him two years ago and moved to Los Angeles. Now she's back."

"Oh, no."

"I don't know what to do. I asked him if he still loved her, and he said he wasn't sure."

Cheryl sighed heavily. She felt bad for Lena, and knew how much Lena was in love with him. Everyone in the office knew. She was surprised, however, to hear this about Quincy. She had gotten the impression from the way he treated Lena around the office, sending her flowers and such, that he felt the same way.

"Lena, don't cry. Come on, honey, don't cry. Listen. Have you seen this woman?" Cheryl asked.

"Yes," Lena answered, as she wiped her eyes. "She came here yesterday to see him."

"What!"

"I thought she was here for an appointment with him."

"Aw, man. Look, you know what you have to do?" Cheryl's mind was working overtime on schemes of vengeance. "You have to find out where she is, even if you have to go to Quincy's house. You let her know, just like you did me, that Quincy is *your* man, and that you're not gonna stand still for her popping up and trying to break up what y'all got. She left him two years ago, so she missed her chance. Tell her to take her ass back to Los Angeles. And then you need to tell Quincy that you're not gonna allow him to be pushing you and pulling you in all directions while he's trying to make up his mind what he wants to do. You know these men don't know what to do. You have to tell them what to do. They're just like children. You tell him to get his act together, or else!"

"I wish I could tell him that like you just said it," Lena told her.

"Honey, when you stop crying and start really thinking about what's goin' on and you start getting angry, you'll tell him. Take my word for it," Cheryl said with conviction.

Lena lowered her head, knowing that despite Cheryl's confidence in her she would never be able to talk to Quincy in that manner. Despite how much more confidence she had in herself now, Lena felt that just walking out of his place had used up all of her strength.

Cheryl smiled sadly and said, "Don't worry, hon, everything'll be all right. Quincy's just having a bit of a lapse, that's all. He's too smart not to realize what a good woman he has in you, even if he's forgotten momentarily. He'll come to his senses soon. You'll see."

"I hope you're right," Lena moaned.

"Don't worry. I'm always right," Cheryl said, trying to make her laugh.

Lena looked into Cheryl's eyes and could not help but smile at her last words.

"Well, most of the time, anyway," Cheryl added with a crooked smile.

"Thanks, Cheryl."

"You're welcome, honey."

Lena met Karen for lunch at ten minutes after one. When she reached the lobby Karen was there waiting for her.

"Hi, Lena," Karen said as they exchanged pecks on the cheek. "You okay?"

"No," Lena admitted.

They walked outside and across the street to the park. Karen had brought a sandwich from home, and Lena told her that she had no appetite, so they took a seat on a park bench and Lena began to tell her what had happened the day before.

"Karen, you know about Quincy's fiancée Rhonda, don't you?"

"Rhonda? What's she got to do with this?"

"She's back."

"What?"

Lena sighed and continued, "She came to the office to see him yesterday."

"What?" Karen repeated.

"He spent last night with her."

"Don't tell me that, Lena," Karen said in exasperation. "Please don't tell me that."

"When he came home this morning and told me, I asked him if he still loves her, and he said he wasn't sure." Her eyes began to water once again.

"Oh my God. No, Quincy, no. How could you be so stupid?" Karen thought aloud.

"Did you know her?"

"Yeah, I knew that witch. He started going with her not too long after I started seeing Serge. I never did like her. Never. I used to pretend for Quincy's sake, 'cause me and Serge used to double date with them all the time, but I couldn't stand her. She used to . . ." Karen sighed. She was clearly vexed by what Lena had told her. "She used him so bad, Lena, and he just let her. He was so crazy in love with her that he couldn't see anything except Rhonda. She could do no wrong. I used to get so angry when I'd hear the way she would talk to him, 'cause Quincy's so sweet. I remember one time, I almost said something to her about it, too, but Serge stopped me. He knew I was gonna go off.

"When she walked out on him . . . I've never seen Quincy like that, and I don't ever want to see anyone like that again. Especially someone I care about. He was devastated. For so long, for weeks, he didn't believe that she had actually left. He used to think she was coming back. Weeks went by. I mean, weeks! He used to talk about her like she was still here, or like she had just gone around the corner to the store or something. When it finally sunk in that she wasn't coming back . . . Aw, man." Karen paused. Lena noticed that Karen's eyes were beginning to water.

"Serge went by to see him. He had been with him all day, and when he left him he came to my house. Serge was in tears. He was so afraid for him. He said Quincy was falling apart. He took a week off from work and stayed cooped up in his apartment by himself. He bought that condo he lives in for them. Then, all of a sudden, he just showed up at Serge's house a week later, and it was as if nothing had ever happened, as if he had blocked the whole thing out of his memory. He never talked about her. He never mentioned her name, or anything. It was as if that part of his life had never happened.

And then he was his old self again. That always scared me, the way he just forgot about it. But he seemed okay.

"You know, when he first met you I saw something in him that I hadn't seen in a long time. He was really happy again. I can't believe that he would let her just . . . just come back and disrupt his life like this all over again. I can't believe it."

"Do you think . . . do you think he still loves her?" Lena asked tearfully.

"I don't think he's even had time to really think about it. You know, about what she did to him." Karen shook her head in disbelief. "Wait until I tell Serge. He's gonna be through."

"I don't want to lose him, Karen," Lena moaned.

Karen put an arm around Lena's shoulder and hugged her. "Don't worry, Lena. He's confused right now. He doesn't know what he's doing."

Tears fell from Lena's eyes as she looked at Karen, praying that she was right about Quincy.

"Oh, Lena, I'm sorry. Don't worry. I'm gonna talk to Serge. He'll talk some sense into him, don't worry."

Karen telephoned Serge immediately upon returning to her office.

"Kinnard! How can I help you?" Serge responded when he picked up the telephone.

"Hi, Serge. It's me," Karen said, solemnly.

"Hey, baby. What's up?"

"Rhonda's back."

"What?"

"You heard me. I just left Lena. She told me that Rhonda came to the job yesterday to see Quincy, and that he spent the night with her last night. He didn't get home until five o'clock this morning."

"Get outta here!"

"Yeah. Lena's a wreck. I met her for lunch, and she just cried and cried."

"I don't believe it. I don't believe it! How could he be so stupid? After what she did to him. What the hell is he thinking about?" Serge said, more to himself than to Karen.

"Can you talk to him?"

"Talk to him? Hmph, I'ma hit him upside his head when I see him," Serge said angrily. "Lena's at work, huh?"

"Yeah. She said she didn't want to stay home because it would leave her too much time to think about what he did."

Serge sucked his teeth. "Is Quincy there?"

"No."

"Let me call this fool. I'll call you back."

"All right."

When Serge hung up, he immediately dialed Quincy's number. When his answering machine picked up, Serge left a bombastic message.

"Yo, Q-man, this is Serge! Where the hell are you? I just got through talking to Karen, and she told me that Rhonda's back in town. What the hell are you doing? I'm coming by there tonight to knock some sense into your thick skull!"

It was a little after noon when Quincy finally dragged himself out of bed. After washing his face and brushing his teeth, he threw on a sweat suit and his sneakers, grabbed his basketball, and headed for the courts.

He needed to think. He did some of his best thinking while he was playing ball.

Quincy returned to his apartment at approximately seven-thirty that evening. He had played ball for almost six hours straight. He was exhausted.

When he stepped off of the elevator on his floor, he was surprised to find Serge standing there.

"Hey, what's up?" Quincy asked.

"Yeah, what the hell is up with you?" Serge said nastily.

Quincy looked at his best friend quizzically and asked, "What do you mean?"

"You know what I mean, man. Don't play dumb."

Quincy moved past Serge and headed for his door.

"I don't know what you're talking about, man," Quincy insisted.

"I'm talking about Rhonda."

Quincy looked at Serge with outright surprise. *How does he know about Rhonda?*

"I know she's back. Lena called Karen, crying about what you did to her for that . . . that . . . witch. Have you forgotten what she did to you?"

"Yo, Serge, I don't want to talk about it, all right?"

"No, it's not all right! Quincy, use your head, man!"

"Look, Serge. I said I don't want to talk about

it! It's my life! I don't need you telling me what to do!"

Serge stood there for a moment without a word. He was hurt that Quincy would not talk to him, and he was afraid for him. Granted, he probably shouldn't have yelled at him that way. But he knew that with Rhonda, Quincy had always been spineless. He was angry that his friend seemed to be setting a trap for himself all over again.

In a voice filled with resignation, Serge said, "Fine. You're right, Q, it is your life. I just have two things I want to say to you, and then I'll leave. Just remember what she did to you the last time, and how easy it was for her to walk away from you. Then think about what you're doing to Lena. Think about how you felt when Rhonda walked out on you, and compare that to what you're doing to that beautiful woman who's always been there for you."

With that, Serge turned and left, opting not to wait for the elevator to take him back downstairs.

Quincy stared at the staircase door Serge had just passed through for a few seconds, then turned and continued toward the door of his apartment.

When he entered the apartment, he dropped his ball and stepped over to his answering machine. There were three messages. He pressed the rewind button and waited for the playback.

The first message was from Serge. The second was from Lena. She was crying freely.

"Quincy, this is Lena. Please call me. I love you."

The sound of her voice tugged at his heartstrings, but he knew he could not call her until he was sure of what he was going to do.

The last message was from Rhonda.

"Hi, Quincy. This is Rhonda. Give me a call when you get in. My mother's goin' out for the night, so you can come over and stay. I'd really like to show you how much I've missed you. Call me when you get in. I love you."

She ended the message with a noisy kissing sound.

He plopped down on his couch, picked up the remote control, and turned on the television. As he sat there, he thought about Rhonda.

He was not sure he was glad she was back, or if he wanted her to go back to LA. He noticed that other than her haircut, she really had not changed much. She was still the same selfish girl he had always loved. He also realized that after he told her about Lena she'd carried on as if he had made no mention of her and continued to try to seduce him, telling him of the things he had to look forward to now that she was back.

Serge did not understand. He was so positive that Quincy had fallen back into Rhonda's arms that he never even considered that he might be trying to make some sense out of his feelings with regard to this whole thing.

Quincy rose from the couch suddenly and went to his hall closet. He reached up to the overhead shelf and pulled down an old boot box that he had shoved up there two years ago. He carried the box back to the sofa and sat down.

He took a deep breath and slowly raised the lid off the box. It was filled almost to the brim with photographs of him and Rhonda. There were pictures of their first vacation together in the Bahamas. There were pictures of the ski trip they had taken, when he fractured his ankle. There were pictures of each and every Christmas they had spent together.

As he looked through them memories of happier times flooded his mind, and he could not help but smile. They had had a lot of fun together, that was for sure.

As the stack of pictures on his coffee table grew and grew, his hand touched a photo of them taken the day he asked her to marry him—Valentine's Day. A semiprofessional photographer had taken the picture outside a movie theater in Times Square. This was his favorite.

He stared at the photograph for almost five minutes before he put it to the side, separating it from the others.

He leaned back on the sofa, resting his head on the back as he gazed up at the ceiling.

The sudden ringing of his telephone startled him. Reluctantly, he began to rise to answer the call, but he decided at the last minute to let it go to his machine.

"Hi, Quincy, it's Rhonda. Where are you? I hope you get this message soon. I'm really horny, and I want to make love to you. Call me. It's an emergency."

That same loud kissing sound followed this message, too.

As he sat there contemplating Rhonda's request, his eyes fell on the white teddy bear that Lena had given him when they went to Great Adventure.

He rose from the sofa and walked over to the étagère where Q-Bear sat. He pulled him down from his perch, and as he studied the fluffy white toy he smiled.

Lena had been so proud of herself playing that water pistol game.

Quincy gently brushed the dust from the bear's surface and returned to the sofa.

"What's up, Q-Bear? Looks like it's just me and you tonight."

He wrapped his arms around the bear, holding it close to his heart as thoughts of Lena filled his brain.

She was the sweetest woman he had ever known. He remembered how shy and timid she had been when they first met, and how different she was now. He smiled when he thought about their first night of love.

He loved making love with her. She was so eager to please him that she did not realize how much she blew his mind with the things she did so innocently. He loved being with her. She had such a pleasant disposition, and she was completely selfless. He loved making her blush, especially in public. She was like a little girl at times, and she made him feel carefree.

Suddenly, the memory of her tears invaded his happy thoughts of her. She did not deserve the hurt he had dealt her. He felt terrible that he had caused her to cry.

Quincy stretched out on the sofa as he held Q-Bear tightly in his grip. A tear fell from his eye as he thought about what he had done to Lena.

"What am I gonna do?" he moaned. He was so confused.

TWENTY-THREE

Lena slept fitfully that night. She had hoped that her telephone would ring, with Quincy calling to tell her how sorry he was and that he wanted her back. To her dismay, the call never came.

When she arose Saturday morning, she was angry. Lena thought about how she had always tried to do everything in her power to please him, and had never asked for anything in return. *How could he do something like this to me?* she asked herself. *He said he loves me. How could he love me and make me suffer like this?*

Suddenly, she remembered the things Cheryl had said to her yesterday. She really did not think she would ever be able to confront Rhonda about Quincy despite her newfound confidence, but the more she thought about it the more she realized that she had to let Quincy know how she felt about the way he had just pushed her aside because his ex had come back to town.

Lena threw the covers back suddenly, and got out of bed. She went to the bathroom and turned on the faucets to take a shower. Lena washed as fast as she could, then stepped out of the tub and dried her body rapidly. She brushed her teeth, then went back to her bedroom and threw on a pair of jeans and an old sweatshirt. She pushed her feet into her sneakers without bothering to put on a pair of socks. Not caring that it was not as neat as it could be, Lena brushed her hair back and tied it in a ponytail with a rubber band. She noticed one of Quincy's baseball caps lying on her dresser, and she grabbed it and carelessly pulled it on her head.

Lena grabbed her keys and wallet from atop her dresser and stuffed the wallet into her jeans pocket. She stomped down the stairs quickly, then grabbed her leather bomber jacket from the front closet and threw it on. She stepped out of the house without a second thought and locked the door, then headed straight for the garage. She unlocked the door of her father's old Cadillac and slid in behind the wheel. As she put the key in the ignition and started the car, she murmured, "I hope you're wearing your body armor, Quincy, 'cause I'm gonna give you a piece of my mind. And she'd better not be there."

Quincy was awakened Saturday morning by the ringing of his telephone. As he sat up on the sofa and stretched to wake himself up, he noticed that Q-Bear had fallen to the floor.

"Sorry, Q-Bear," he said as he picked the fluffy toy up from the floor and brushed it off.

The phone rang a fourth time, and although

he got up to answer it he waited to see who it
was before he picked up the receiver.

"Quincy, it's Rhonda. Are you there?"

He lifted the receiver from its base and spoke.
"Hey, Rhonda."

"Hi. Were you asleep?"

"Yeah, but that's all right. I need to get up,
anyway."

"Did you get my messages last night? I was
hoping you would come over."

"It was too late when I got in," he lied.

"Do you have company now?"

"No."

"Can I come over?"

"Yeah, come on," he said without hesitation.

"Great. I'll be there in about thirty minutes."

"All right. I'll be here."

When he had hung up the phone, Quincy
lumbered to the bathroom. He turned on the
shower, stripped off his clothes, then grabbed
his toothbrush and toothpaste and stepped into
the stall. As he stood under the spray, he
brushed his teeth.

He felt good, better than he had in the past
two days. His head was clear. He knew what he
had to do. There was no more second-guessing.

When Quincy got out of the shower, he dried
himself and went into his bedroom to get
dressed. He splashed on a generous amount of
Calvin Klein's CK One. Although he was not getting dressed up, he took special care with his
grooming. He had some very important things
to do.

Once he was dressed he returned to the living

room and began to clean up the mess he had made while going through his box of photos. He picked up the one of him and Rhonda that he loved and placed it on the étagère with his basketball trophies.

He replaced the lid on the box and picked it up from the table. It was time to bury the past. *The future is now,* he reasoned, and he realized that he could not look back.

He walked into his kitchen and lifted the lid of his garbage can. Quincy dumped the box into the can, then walked back to his living room and turned on the stereo.

Something mellow, he decided. Something to set the mood. He decided on Spyro Gyra's *Got The Magic.*

When Rhonda hung up the phone after talking to Quincy, she headed straight for the door. She had gotten up early, disappointed about not being able to spend the night with him. She wondered if he had been with that girl he was seeing. She hoped he had told her it was over.

She knew Quincy still loved her, even though he had not come right out and said it. She was sure that once he realized how much she still loved him, he would forgive her and take her back with open arms.

"Mom, I'm going over to Quincy's. I probably won't be back until real late," Rhonda told her mother before she left.

When she stepped out of her building, she was in luck. There was a cab dropping someone

off right across the street. She ran to catch it
before it pulled away.

She was at Quincy's apartment thirty-five minutes later.

As soon as she stepped into the building, she
got a feeling of déjà vu. She remembered when
they had come here to look at the apartment
Quincy now lived in. The lobby was as beautiful
as it had been then.

The doorman called upstairs to announce her
arrival. When she stepped onto the elevator, she
was smiling. She was glad she'd decided to come
back home, and she was glad she had come back
to Quincy. When she really thought about it, she
had to admit he was the best thing that had ever
happened to her.

When his doorbell rang, Quincy was in the
kitchen fixing himself a light breakfast of toast
with apple butter and tea. He opened the refrigerator and placed the apple butter on the
shelf before he went to answer the door.

He was wiping his hands on a napkin when
he let Rhonda in.

"Hi!" she said, cheerfully. She wrapped him
in a warm embrace and placed a sensuous kiss
on his lips.

"Hi."

"How are you?"

She walked into the apartment and began to
remove her jacket as if she belonged there.

"I'm all right. How're you doing?"

"Better now," she said with a mischievous smile.

"I was just fixing myself a couple of pieces of toast. Can I get you anything?"

"No, I already ate." She looked around the apartment. She had not been there since he first moved in. "I like what you've done with the place," she said sincerely.

"Thanks."

Quincy moved back to the kitchen to get his breakfast.

"So, what's up?" she asked as she examined his trophies and other knickknacks.

"Not much. What's up with you?"

"Other than the fact that I'm horny as hell, nothing."

Quincy chuckled, but did not respond.

"Ow wow! I remember this," Rhonda declared.

"What's that?" Quincy asked, although he knew what she was referring to.

"This picture of us. This is the night you proposed to me," she said in a dulcet tone.

"Yup, you're right."

"That was a beautiful night."

"Yeah, it was nice."

Quincy brought his toast into the living room and set the dish on the coffee table. He returned to the kitchen to get his tea.

"Would you like some tea, Rhonda?"

"No, thanks."

When he returned, he sat on the couch and placed his mug on the table in front of him. He reached for a slice of the toast and took a big bite.

Rhonda was standing by his wall unit and looking at him with a silly smile on her face.

"What?" he asked, with his mouth full.

"Nothing." She sighed, then said, "That's not true. It's just that . . . well, I never realized how much I missed you until I got back and saw you again."

"I missed you too, Rhonda," Quincy said as he continued to eat his breakfast.

She moved over to the couch and took a seat beside him.

"I'm sorry I left you the way I did. It was just that, at the time I felt that was my only chance. You know how much I wanted to do that. I felt that if I didn't do it while I could, I'd always be wondering what if?"

"I understand, Rhonda," he said calmly.

"I'm glad you don't hate me, though. I was afraid you might."

Quincy smiled and thought for a moment before he answered. "I loved you too much to hate you. I just wish you'd called me, or written. I could never understand why you didn't."

"I know. I was afraid that if I called you you would hang up on me, and if I wrote my letters would come back unopened. After I found out what a creep Ray was, I was really too afraid to call anyone, including my mother."

Quincy listened closely to what she said. He thought about it for a moment, then decided to tell her everything that happened when she left. He needed to tell her. He felt it would be the only way he could put that part of his life behind him and move on.

"It was hard for me when you left, Rhonda. I couldn't believe you were actually gone. I kept thinking that you would ring that bell and tell me that you had changed your mind about leaving. Weeks went by, and I still didn't want to believe it. Serge used to tell me that I was waiting for you in vain, but I wouldn't hear him. I used to tell him that he didn't know you like I did. I used to tell him that you wouldn't do that to me."

Rhonda was silent throughout Quincy's narrative. She listened intently to everything he said. She was finding out, for the first time, how much she had actually hurt him.

Quincy was surprisingly calm as he spoke. For him, the worst was over.

He rose from the couch and took his breakfast dishes into the kitchen and placed them in the sink. Then he returned to the living room and sat beside her again.

"You know, Rhonda, I hate to admit this, but I almost had a nervous breakdown when you left. When I finally realized that you were not coming back, I was devastated. I didn't want to live. Not if I couldn't have you. I'm not proud of it, but for a moment I even thought about . . ." He paused for a moment, then shook his head. "Never mind. I really lost it. But I realize now what it was that I had done wrong. You were my whole life, Rhonda. You were everything. I walked and talked and breathed you. I loved you more than I loved myself, and that's where I went wrong. The only thing that mattered to me was you.

"I couldn't accept your leaving, so I acted like it had never happened. That was how I was able to get on with my life. I just blocked it out. But that wasn't the answer, either. Denial is never good. It's not therapeutic. When you showed up at my office the other day, I panicked. Honestly. Why do you think I sent my secretary out there to get you? I didn't think I could even face you. I wasn't ready to deal with the part of my life that I had pushed to the back of my mind," Quincy explained.

He rose from the couch just then and slowly stepped over to the window. His back was to her as he continued.

"I've never loved anyone the way I loved you, Rhonda. I don't think I ever will again, because I've learned how to love myself."

He turned back to her. He had a very peaceful smile on his face.

"It took a very long time for me to get you out of my system, and when you showed up the other day I realized that I really hadn't. I—"

At that moment, the ringing of his doorbell interrupted him.

"Are you expecting anyone?" she asked.

"Nope. Excuse me a minute."

Quincy walked to the door, slightly irritated that he had been interrupted during the most significant speech of his life.

Lena had stood outside Quincy's door for almost five minutes before she found the courage to ring the bell, knowing there was no turning back. She had to say what was on her mind, regardless of the outcome. She knew this was the true test of her strength of character and pride. She also realized that it was very possible that she might lose him in the next couple of minutes, but that was a chance she had decided to take.

She had taken a deep breath and pressed the button. The door was opened almost immediately.

"Lena!" Quincy said in amazement when he saw her standing there.

"I have to talk to you, Quincy. It's very important," she said firmly.

"I was going to call you. Come inside," he said as he opened the door wider to let her in.

Lena stepped into the apartment, prepared to tell him off. Then she noticed Rhonda sitting on his couch. She stopped in her tracks; the pain of knowing that she had lost him to this woman was more than she could bear. She looked up at Quincy, and all of her resolve faded. Her eyes began to water, and she turned away from him and headed back out the door.

Quincy immediately noticed the pained look on her face, and as she was stepping out of the apartment he grabbed her. "Lena, wait."

"No, no! Let me go, Quincy! Let me go!" she cried.

She tried to pull away from him, but he was too strong for her.

"Lena, wait. It's not what you think."

"No! Leave me alone!"

She continued to struggle until he stepped

out of the apartment with her and wrapped his arms around her.

"It's not what you think. Lena, I love you. I don't want anyone else. I want you, angel," Quincy insisted.

"Then what is she doing here?"

"Lena, listen. Listen to me. Stop crying, sweetheart. Please, stop crying. Come inside with me."

"No!"

"Please come inside with me," he pleaded, softly. "I love you, angel, and I'm sorry for hurting you. I'm so sorry. I don't want anyone but you, Lena."

"What is she doing here?" Lena repeated.

"Come inside with me, and I'll explain everything."

"No! You explain it now, because I don't want to be here with her."

"She's not staying," Quincy continued in the same gentle tone.

"Why is she here at all? Did she spend the night with you?"

"No, Lena."

"Then why?"

"I was . . . I needed to see her so I could tell her how I felt about what she did to me."

"Why couldn't you tell her that the other night? You were with her all night."

"I was confused."

"How do I know you're not confused now? How do I know you won't decide later that she's the one you really want?"

"I'm not confused now, angel. I've never been more sure of anything in my life," he said gently.

Lena did not comment.

Quincy continued, "I love you, Lena Caldwell. I have no more doubts. Please have faith in me. I know I don't have the right to ask you for anything, but please understand that I have to do this. I have to bring this to a close."

She looked into his eyes with anger and confusion, but she could see the love he so staunchly professed. As Quincy hugged her close to him, he could feel her body relax in his embrace.

"Come on," he said. He took her hand and slowly led her back into his apartment.

Once they were inside, he continued to hold her hand. It was sheer determination that helped Lena check the flow of tears from her eyes. She absolutely refused to let this woman see her cry.

Quincy said, "Rhonda, you remember Lena, don't you? She's the receptionist at my office."

As Rhonda sat on the couch and watched Quincy with Lena, she slowly came to realize what he was trying to do. "Yes," she murmured hesitantly.

He released Lena's hand and put his arm around her waist. "She's also the woman who was here the night I was with you."

To Lena, he whispered, "Sit down, sweetheart."

"I'd rather stand, thank you," she said, as she looked up at him angrily, then turned her attention to Rhonda.

"All right." Quincy turned his attention back to Rhonda. "You see, Rhonda, this is what I was trying to tell you. When we were together, there was nothing that I wouldn't have done for you. Nothing. And you knew that. I think that's why you came back. I think you expected to find the same old Quincy. But I've changed. I'm not that man anymore." As Rhonda sat there and Quincy's words began to sink in, her heart started to break, and her eyes began to water.

"This lady here . . . she's my best friend. I love her, and she loves me. And I trust her to never hurt me the way you did, to never walk out on me, to never turn her back on me. And I feel very bad . . . I feel very small, because I almost did to her what you did to me."

Quincy then turned to face Lena and told her, "I'm sorry I hurt you, Lena. I'm sorry I put you through that. I hope you'll be able to forgive me, because I promise it will never happen again."

Lena stared into Quincy's eyes for a moment. Then she briefly turned to look over at Rhonda, who stared straight ahead, her face lined with tears. Lena almost felt sorry for her.

She looked back into Quincy's eyes for a few seconds before she spoke softly. "I forgive you."

He embraced her briefly and brushed her forehead with a kiss before he turned back to his ex. "Rhonda, I've finally been able to get on with my life. I don't regret any of the time we spent together, the years we had, but that part of my life is over. It's time to move on. I thank you for all those times—the good times and the bad times, too, I guess, 'cause it's all of that that makes us who we are. But I realize, too, that if you hadn't come back I wouldn't have known this.'' Tears fell from Rhonda's eyes as she looked up at him. "We can't hold on to the past, Rhonda, because it's gone. You're a beautiful woman with your whole life ahead of you. It's time for you to start living it. I can't be a part of your life anymore. Our time is over, and life goes on.''

Quincy shrugged his shoulders. He felt, honestly, that there was nothing else he could say.

Rhonda was crushed. She had realized too late just how important he really was to her.

When she was finally able to collect herself enough to rise from the sofa, she walked toward the door and past him, without a word. When she had her hand on the doorknob and had opened the door, she turned back to him and said, "I'm sorry, Quincy. Good-bye.''

He did not move. He did not turn to her. That part of his life was over. When he heard the door close behind her, he felt as though a weight had been lifted from his shoulders; a weight he had not realized he was carrying until she came back.

Lena moved away from him when she heard the door close, and stepped over to the window. Tears streamed down her face. Quincy looked over at her back. After a few seconds, he walked over and joined her at the window. He stood behind her and wrapped his arms around her as he softly whispered, "I know you said you'd forgive me, but I know you're still angry, and I understand."

Lena remained silent.

Quincy was struggling to find the right words to say to her. He became choked up thinking about the last couple of days, and how he had put their relationship in jeopardy by not using his head. Tears fell from his eyes as he said, "I can't believe I let myself forget how important you are to me."

Lena turned to face him, then. She looked up into his eyes for a moment before she reached up to wipe his tears away. "I think I understand what you were going through. I mean, she was a part of your life for a long time, and you never had the chance to tell her what you felt. Just answer one question for me, though. Is there anyone else who's going to come and try to take you from me again?"

"No, Lena. There's no one else. Oh, baby," Quincy said emotionally. "I love you so much. I'm so sorry."

Lena embraced him tightly and cried, "I love you, Quincy."

Quincy looked into her eyes, kissed her tears from her face, and told her, "I want to spend the rest of my life with you, Lena. Will you marry me? Will you be my wife?"

Lena smiled through her tears as she softly whispered, "Yes, Quincy, I'll marry you."

Their lips met in a passionate kiss filled with love and hope and all the good things they felt in their hearts.

TWENTY-FOUR

Serge had been awake since seven-thirty Saturday morning. He'd lain there thinking about Quincy, genuinely worried about him. He sincerely hoped that Quincy would not allow himself to be taken in by Rhonda again.

He felt bad for Lena, too. He had come to love Lena, and thought she was the perfect woman for Quincy. Her love for him was true. Serge knew that without a doubt. He also knew, from what Karen had told him and from knowing the type of person she was, that she was crushed by this.

Serge had to admit that he had gone about it the wrong way in confronting Quincy. He figured he probably should not have jumped on his case the way he did, but should have tried to talk to him like a man. But he had been trying to protect his friend. Knowing what a nice guy Quincy was, and knowing the way he had always felt about her, he was sure that Rhonda's sweet talking would woo him once again.

Suddenly, Serge had sat up on the bed and put his feet on the floor. He leaned over and—while resting his elbows on his lap—put his head in his hands.

His movements had awakened Karen. When she saw his defeated posture, she'd asked, "What's wrong, Serge?"

He'd sat straight up and turned to her. "Oh, hi, baby. I'm sorry if I woke you."

"You didn't. What's the matter?"

"I was just thinking about Quincy."

"You're really worried about him, aren't you?"

"Yeah. I just keep thinking about how he was when she left him before, and I know she'll do it again without a second thought."

"Do you really think he still loves her?"

"I don't know. He damn near tore my head off yesterday when I tried to talk to him about her."

"Yeah, but you said you were kind of rough with him."

"I know, but when he said, 'it's my life,' I just got the feeling that he was gonna take her back."

"Do you really think he could just brush Lena aside like that?"

"I would have never thought so before, but I'm not sure now. You know how he was with Rhonda. You know he would do anything for her, regardless of what anyone thought."

"I know."

They were both silent for a few minutes or so, thinking about their friend.

"You know, Serge, Lena told me that Quincy is the only man she's ever been with."

"I know. Quincy told me that a while ago."

"She really loves him."

"I know she does. I thought he loved her, too."

After a few more minutes of silence, Serge rose from the bed and said, "I'm gonna go try to talk to him again."

"Let me come with you. Maybe if we both talk to him and remind him of what he's got now with Lena, he'll see that he's making a mistake."

"All right. Come on, let's get dressed."

"Did you eat anything, baby?" Quincy asked Lena as they sat together on his couch later that morning.

"No, but I'm not really hungry."

She was snuggled in his arms, and a feeling of bliss emanated from them.

Lena was happy Quincy had chosen her over Rhonda, but she knew that he must have struggled with his choice. She could not help but ask, "You really loved her, didn't you?"

"Lena."

"It's all right, Quincy. I don't mind talking about her. I'm not worried about her anymore."

He kissed her softly on her cheek. "I've always said it, and I still believe it. You're one in a million," Quincy said with a smile.

She gazed up at him and smiled.

"Yeah, I did, Lena," he said reminiscently.

"You told her that you thought the reason she came back was that she knew you had always loved her and would probably take her back, but I think she really loved you, too."

"Yeah, I never doubted that she did, but

Rhonda is selfish. She always has been. Even when we were together, everything had to be done her way. I was just so blind with love that I overlooked that and went along with it."

"Do you think she'll go back to LA?"

"No."

"Do you think she'll call you again and try to see you?"

"No, I don't."

"What if she does?"

"The guesswork is over. I don't love her anymore. I love you. With you is where I want to be."

"Quincy, I don't want you to think that I doubt what you're saying, or that I doubt your love, but when you were with her Thursday night, where did you go?"

"To dinner and the movies."

"That's all?"

"Uh-huh."

"But—"

"We walked around in the Village for a while, and that's about it."

"Did you make love to her?"

"No, Lena, I didn't. That's the truth. I promised I would never be unfaithful to you, and I plan to keep that promise now and forever."

She looked into his eyes and saw no trace of falsehood.

"Now, I'll admit that I had a momentary lapse, but I never forgot my promise to you. I never stopped loving you, angel. As sweet as you are, I don't think I ever will."

"You don't have to say that just to make me feel good."

"I'm not. Have I ever patronized you?"

"No."

"And I'm not about to start now. I can't deny that while I was first with Rhonda I was glad she was back, but I couldn't get you out of my mind. I told her about you. I told her that what we had was serious. She acted like I'd never said a word. But that's how she is, selfish. She had pretty much made up her mind that she was going to have me again, that things were going to be the way they used to be. But yesterday when I got up, I went out and played some ball and I thought about everything. When I came home Serge was waiting for me, and he was pissed off about me spending the night with her. See, he was there when she left. I didn't want to talk to him, though, 'cause I had to make up my own mind about what I wanted to do with my life. I was here all night. I got your message yesterday, and it killed me to listen to you crying like that, but I didn't call you because I had to be one hundred percent sure about how I felt about her."

"You know, when I came here this morning, I had every intention of telling you off," Lena confessed.

"I can't say as I blame you."

"Cheryl saw me in the bathroom at work yesterday, and I told her what happened. She told me to tell you off. I didn't think I could, but when I woke up this morning and you still hadn't called, I got angry. She told me if I got angry, I would do it."

"Cheryl's a trip. She likes you, though," Quincy said with a smile.

"She likes you, too," Lena said with a chuckle.

Quincy had to laugh, also.

"She's funny," he said. "You know, Lena, I'm glad I've got you. I'm glad that we have what we have. I went to sleep right here with Q-Bear last night, and when I woke up, I realized that I would have to be stupid to give you up. I might be a little slow sometimes, but I'm not stupid."

He kissed her softly on her lips and gazed into her eyes.

"I love you, Lena."

"I love you, Quincy."

They kissed again, this time with overwhelming passion as Quincy's embrace tightened.

As they sat there in a seemingly impenetrable embrace, the doorbell rang.

"Damn! Who the hell is that?" Quincy groaned as he and Lena separated.

She laughed and said, "You've had a lot of traffic this morning, huh?"

"No kidding."

"Well, whoever it is, get rid of 'em. I wanna go to bed," she said seductively.

Quincy smiled at her as he rose from the couch and headed to the door. "They're as good as gone."

When he opened the door, he was surprised to see Serge and Karen standing there.

"What's up, man?" Serge said humbly.

Karen smiled and said, "Hi."

"Hi, Karen," Quincy said. He simply stared at Serge.

Serge bowed his head for a brief moment before he said, "Look, I'm sorry about yesterday. Do you mind if we come in?"

"Is that Karen and Serge?" Lena called as she rose from the couch and started toward the door.

Quincy pulled the door open for them to enter.

"Hi, Lena," Karen said with a big smile.

"Hi." Lena was smiling like the cat who swallowed the canary. "Hi, Serge."

"Hey, Lena. How you doin'?" Serge asked.

"Fine."

Serge could not help but smile at the look of sheer joy on Lena's face.

Karen walked into the living room with Lena, but Serge and Quincy remained near the front door.

"I guess I put my foot in my mouth, huh?" Serge said.

"I told you I would work it out for myself."

"I was worried about you, okay?"

Quincy and Serge had been friends for many years and they'd had many arguments and disagreements before. Quincy had always attributed that to the fact that that was just how brothers were.

"Look, I know you were worried. I was, too, for a while, but this was something that I had to do by myself. You understand that, don't you?"

"Yeah, I understand."

"I appreciate the fact that you were tryin' to look out for me," Quincy admitted.

"Hey, ain't no thing, man," Serge said, his hand extended in brotherhood.

Quincy took his hand, but also embraced Serge, thankful that he had a friend like him.

To the Reader:

Thank you for your continued support and for taking the time out of your busy schedule to read my story, *First Love*. I hope you've enjoyed meeting Lena and Quincy. They are two of my favorite characters, and I hope they have found their way into your heart, as well.

I'd love to hear your comments on the story, so please feel free to e-mail me with your thoughts. My address is Faye1257@aol.com. Looking forward to hearing from you. In the meantime, keep love in your heart and everyday will be beautiful.

Cheryl Faye

ABOUT THE AUTHOR

In addition to *First Love,* Cheryl Faye has published three romance novels and a short story for Arabesque: *At First Sight, A Time for Us,* and *A Test Of Time* and "Second Chance At Love" in the anthology *Mama Dear.* She is currently employed as a legal secretary at a major New York law firm. Cheryl is the proud mother of two fine sons, Michael, 24, and Douglas, 13. She currently resides in Wappingers Falls, NY, with her fiancé.

Coming in September from Arabesque Books . . .

TRUE LOVE by Brenda Jackson
1-58314-144-8 $5.99US/$7.99CAN
When Shayla Kirkland lands her dream job with one of Chicago's top firms, Chenault Electronics, she's in the perfect position to destroy the company for ruining her mother's career. But she never expects that CEO Nicholas Chenault will spark a passion that will challenge her resolve—and make her surrender to the most irresistible desire . . .

ENDLESS LOVE by Carmen Green
1-58314-135-9 $5.99US/$7.99CAN
Terra O'Shaughssey always did everything as carefully as she could—including managing an apartment building. But when handsome lawyer Michael Crawford becomes her newest tenant, Terra finds his party ways endangering her peace of mind . . . and her carefully shielded heart.

STOLEN MOMENTS by Dianne Mayhew
1-58314-119-7 $5.99US/$7.99CAN
Although widowed Sionna Michaels dreads confronting the man she holds responsible for her husband's death, the instant she sees David Young, her heart is set afire and she's certain of his innocence. There's only one obstacle in the couple's way—the truth about what really happened.

LOVE UNDERCOVER by S. Tamara Sneed
1-58314-142-1 $5.99US/$7.99CAN
When executive Jessica Larson meets FBI anti-terrorist agent Carey Riley in a remote mountain inn, she gives in to her most sensuous desires for the first time in her life. But when a dangerous enemy begins to watch their every move, the two must face down their doubts and fears about getting close . . . if they are to gain a love beyond all they've ever imagined.

Please Use the Coupon on the Next Page to Order

Fall In Love With
Arabesque Books

__TRUE LOVE by Brenda Jackson
    1-58314-144-8 $5.99US/$7.99CAN

__ENDLESS LOVE by Carmen Green
    1-58314-135-9 $5.99US/$7.99CAN

__STOLEN MOMENTS by Dianne Mayhew
    1-58314-119-7 $5.99US/$7.99CAN

__LOVE UNDERCOVER by S. Tamara Sneed
    1-58314-142-1 $5.99US/$7.99CAN

Call toll free **1-888-345-BOOK** to order by phone or use this coupon to order by mail. *ALL BOOKS AVAILABLE SEPTEMBER 1, 2000.*

Name_____

Address_____

City_____ State _____ Zip _____

Please send me the books I have checked above.

I am enclosing $_____

Plus postage and handling* $_____

Sales tax (in NY, TN, and DC) $_____

Total amount enclosed $_____

*Add $2.50 for the first book and $.50 for each additional book.

Send check or money order (no cash or CODs) to: **Arabesque Books, Dept. C.O., 850 Third Avenue, 16th Floor, New York, NY 10022**

Prices and numbers subject to change without notice.

All orders subject to availability.

Visit our website at **www.arabesquebooks.com**